Books by

CAROLYN KEENE

Nancy Drew Mystery Stories

The Secret of the Old Clock
The Hidden Staircase
The Bungalow Mystery
The Mystery at Lilac Inn
The Secret at Shadow Ranch
The Secret of Red Gate Farm
The Clue in the Diary
Nancy's Mysterious Letter
The Sign of the Twisted Candles
The Password to Larkspur Lane
The Clue of the Broken Locket
The Message in the Hollow Oak
The Mystery of the Ivory Charm
The Whispering Statue
The Haunted Bridge
The Clue of the Tapping Heels

The Mystery of the Brass Bound Trunk
The Mystery at the Moss-Covered Mansion
The Quest of the Missing Map
The Clue in the Jewel Box
The Secret in the Old Attic
The Clue in the Crumbling Wall
The Mystery of the Tolling Bell
The Clue in the Old Album
The Ghost of Blackwood Hall
The Clue of the Leaning Chimney
The Secret of the Wooden Lady
The Clue of the Black Keys
The Mystery at the Ski Jump
The Clue of the Velvet Mask

Dana Girls Mystery Stories

By the Light of the Study Lamp
The Secret at Lone Tree Cottage
In the Shadow of the Tower
A Three-Cornered Mystery
The Secret at the Hermitage
The Circle of Footprints
The Mystery of the Locked Room

The Clue in the Cobweb
The Secret at the Gatehouse
The Mysterious Fireplace
The Clue of the Rusty Key
The Portrait in the Sand
The Secret in the Old Well
The Clue in the Ivy

The Secret of the Jade Ring

NANCY HAD AN EXCELLENT VIEW OF HIM AS HE
DASHED DOWN THE STAIRS.
Nancy's Mysterious Letter

NANCY'S MYSTERIOUS LETTER

BY

CAROLYN KEENE

NEW YORK
GROSSET & DUNLAP
PUBLISHERS

CONTENTS

iii

iv   Contents

CHAPTER I

The Stolen Mail

•"Home again!" Nancy Drew spoke as she stopped her sporty maroon roadster before the walk of her own house.

"We have had a wonderful ride," said Bess Marvin, "and we thank you lots and lots." George Fayne, her cousin, nodded in agreement.

The three chums of long standing were returning from an outing at Red Gate Farm, where old Mrs. Burd had loaded the car with farm produce.

"We always have such good times at the farm," exclaimed Nancy, "that I certainly hate to leave, and they are so generous, too. Just look at the stuff we have!"

The girls began unloading the car. Nancy's pretty face was half hidden by the sprays of celery protruding from a big paper bag she now clasped in her arms. A pair of dressed ducks which she held between her fingers nearly slipped from her grasp, and in rescuing them she dropped a glove.

"I'll carry the popcorn ears," offered the plump Bess, who loved good things to eat. She retrieved the glove and returned it. "And the big pumpkin, too," she added.

"I'll take the eggs," offered George, "and the potatoes, and the apples, and everything that is left."

The three girls laughed merrily. It was at Red Gate Farm that Nancy had solved one of her most interesting and thrilling mysteries with her chums. It was pleasant for them to return there occasionally and see how they had improved the place with their original ideas.

"I guess that's all now," pointed out Bess as the boyish George, balancing the eggs and potatoes, backed away from the car directly into Nancy.

For a moment a catastrophe threatened as each girl strove to right her bundles at the unexpected collision.

"My goodness! What a pudding we would have made if we'd fallen down!" exclaimed George. "I'll be glad if I get this load into your house safely."

The girls followed the winding walk that crossed the lawn of the attractive Drew residence. The house door was opened by Hannah Gruen, the middle-aged housekeeper.

"Gracious! Why didn't you call me?" she cried. "Here, give me something."

"Just see that there aren't any wrinkles in the rugs, or any footstools in the way and we will take this stuff right into the pantry."

The girls marched through the rooms to the rear of the house, carrying bundle after bundle.

"I guess I'll have to unload you," laughed Hannah Gruen. "My, what lovely young ducks. Such tender birds. And such a lot of eggs! Can you put the pumpkin on the floor?"

"Phew! My arms are stiff," Nancy said, stretching them as she deposited the last of her supplies. "Has the mail come yet?"

"No, not yet. Unless there was none for us and old Dixon went by."

"Expecting a letter, Nancy?" drawled George, winking at her cousin.

"No, but——"

"Then you must have heard from Ned Nickerson in yesterday's mail," George said innocently.

"Ned Nickerson? Why, he doesn't write——" Nancy began. Then, seeing that she was being teased, she added hastily, "he telegraphs!"

"Has he telegraphed you any football tickets yet?" Bess asked.

"Oh, be serious now," Nancy protested good

humoredly. "I don't want to miss Mr. Dixon. He has brought letters here all my life. I think that I have known him longer than anybody else except Dad, and now he is going to retire."

"Retire!" exclaimed George, following Nancy and Bess into the living room. "Fancy a letter-carrier retiring! I didn't know they were paid well enough to save up a fortune."

"Oh, they get a pension, you know," Nancy said. "But the thrilling part of it is that Mr. Dixon really has a fortune. It's a little one, but he has just inherited it from an ancient aunt out West, and now he is going to retire and raise guinea pigs."

"Guinea pigs!" chorused the cousins.

"Yes, he's an enthusiast already," Nancy laughed. "He told me—oh, there's the 'phone. Excuse me a minute, girls."

Nancy crossed the hall into the library and took down the receiver.

"Hello, is this you, Miss Drew? This is Mrs. Van Ness."

"Good afternoon, Mrs. Van Ness," Nancy replied, recognizing the name as that of a woman living a couple of blocks distant.

"Mr. Dixon, our letter man, left here a few minutes ago. You have heard of his good fortune, I suppose? Yes? It occurred to me that if all of us on his route would contribute a couple of dollars we could present him with a purse or some little gift as a farewell remembrance from those he has served so faithfully."

"Why, I'd be delighted, and so will my father," Nancy replied. "It is a splendid idea, Mrs. Van Ness. I'll bring you a check this very day."

Nancy reported the conversation to her friends and went on to tell them more about the faithful mail carrier.

"He has been in the service for thirty-five years, he told me, and in all that time he has not had a single complaint against him, nor has he lost a letter," Nancy said. "Just think! Why, he must have handled millions of letters in all sorts of weather during that time."

"Well, I certainly hope his record isn't marred the last day or two," George said pessimistically.

"Aren't you the cheerful thing!" Bess cried.

At this point Hannah entered the room, her broad face beaming above a tray loaded with good things.

"I thought the sharp air might have given you an appetite," she said. "So I made some cocoa and here are some fancy cakes I baked after a recipe on the baking powder can."

"Hannah Gruen, that's great!" exclaimed Nancy, quickly drawing up a coffee table.

"And to think I'm dieting," moaned Bess. "Cocoa and sweet cakes are off my list, but only after this afternoon. Then I'll start all over again.''

The housekeeper left the girls to serve themselves. Nancy had filled only one cup with the hot beverage when to her ears came the cheery trill of the mailman's whistle.

"There's Mr. Dixon now," she said, putting down the cocoa pot. "I'll ask him in to share our treat."

George and Bess lived in another part of town and did not know the fortunate mailman who was putting aside his pouch to become a guinea pig fancier. It was with some curiosity, then, that they awaited his coming.

"Hello, Miss Nancy!"

George and Bess noticed the greeting, given in a courteous, cheerful voice.

"How are you, Mr. Dixon?" Nancy was heard to respond. "Won't you come in for a cup of hot cocoa and some brand new little cakes?"

"Well, now," chuckled the mailman, "I don't know but that I'll stop just long enough for a cookie, but business before pleasure. Here's your mail."

"Why, a letter from England!" Nancy said. "How funny, I don't know anyone in England. But come in, Mr. Dixon, do!"

"I don't know as I should," Mr. Dixon said. "It isn't strictly according to regulations."

George and Bess rose from their chairs as Nancy entered the room, leading by the hand one of the most likable-looking elderly men either had ever seen. His ruddy cheeks, the network of "grin wrinkles" (as Nancy called them) at the corners of his bright blue eyes, the close-clipped white moustache and crisp white hair, made of Ira Dixon a man anyone would notice.

Introductions were made and gracefully acknowledged.

"Here is your cocoa," Nancy said. "I'll put a couple of cakes on the saucer, so you won't have to balance a plate."

"I won't sit down, if you'll excuse me," Dixon said. "I left my mail, pouch and all, on the porch and I'll just stand here, because I can't stay very long."

Nancy looked longingly at her letter, which she had propped against the sugar bowl on the tray. A letter from Europe was something she did not often receive, and she was tempted to be impolite enough to discover its secret.

"I was telling the girls about your good luck," she said to the postman, turning her eyes from the long, crisp envelope. "And about the guinea pigs."

"I suppose you don't know much about guinea pigs," Dixon smiled, turning to George and Bess. "Funny thing, they aren't pigs and

don't come from Guinea, either. I suppose you
know that if you pick one up by the tail his
eyes will drop out.''

The three girls gasped.

"Oh, how awful!" Bess cried. "Please don't
try it with any of yours, Mr. Dixon."

Dixon laughed so hard his cocoa nearly
spilled.

"That's just a joke," he explained.
"Guinea pigs have no tails, no more than they
have wings."

"I told my friends about your many years
of service with a perfect record," Nancy said,
after the laughter died down.

"Yes, both as man and boy, I've worked for
Uncle Sam," Dixon said more soberly. "I'll
be glad to give my feet a rest. I guess I've
walked 50,000 miles delivering good news and
bad. Speaking of bad news, Miss Nancy, I've
had some myself."

"Oh, not about your inheritance——?"

Dixon nodded.

"I have a half-brother you don't know about,
named Edgar. Aunt Letitia was no kin of his,
being a sister of my mother, you see, and
Edgar is my step-mother's son. But he is a
sort of black sheep, a wild boy he always was,
and now he is claiming a part of my little fortune.''

Nancy, who had been eyeing her mysterious

letter with growing curiosity, looked up at the mailman.

"Of course he can't get any part of it legally!" she said, indignation in her voice.

"I suppose not," Dixon said. "I don't know for sure. But he can certainly worry me a lot. If only he had asked me in a nice way, but he started threatening me from the start. Maybe I ought to share my money with him."

"I wouldn't do it!" the girls chorused.

"Well, well, here I am chatting away as if I were on the retired list already," the mailman smiled. "I must be on my way. Thank you for the refreshments and for being kind to an old man."

Dixon turned to the door.

Nancy felt half ashamed to admit to herself the fact that she was not averse to having the letter-carrier go, for she was eager to read her English letter. She went to the door and held it open for Dixon.

"Good day, Miss Nancy," he said. "I hope you will come and—why, I must have left my pouch inside. I'm getting forgetful."

"No, I think you left it here by the door," Nancy answered, bewildered. "I'll look, though."

Nowhere in the hall or living room could the worn leather pouch or any of its trusted contents be seen.

"Did I leave it on the steps?" muttered Dixon, his hands shaking and a waxen pallor spreading over his face. "No, it isn't anywhere. It's stolen! I'm ruined! After all these years of perfect service!"

CHAPTER II

"You Are to Blame!"

The mail bag was certainly gone—stolen!

Dixon sank down upon the porch steps, his face buried in his trembling hands.

Nancy looked down at the broken old man with pity and remorse. If only she had not invited him into her home!

"I'll run to the neighbors and see if they saw anyone acting suspiciously around here," she offered.

Dixon made no answer. Bess and George stood in the doorway, not fully comprehending what the trouble was.

Nancy cut across the lawn and through the leafless shrubbery to the house next door, but no one was at home. Then she remembered that these neighbors had gone to California for the winter, and, chiding herself for the delay, she cut across to the house on the other side of her home. There a maid answered the door and said that no one was in the house but herself, and she had been busy in the kitchen. Dixon had not yet reached that residence.

11

Across the street Nancy flew, and tugged at the old-fashioned door pull of a venerable mansion.

After what seemed to her an endless delay the door was opened by a brawny woman redolent of yellow soap and with bubbles from the washtub's suds fresh on her arms.

"Somebody?" she asked.

"Is anyone at home?" Nancy demanded. "The mailman's pouch has been stolen. Did you see anybody sneaking around here?"

The woman grimaced and shrugged her shoulders.

"Not speak Engulsh, me," she smiled. "You speak maybe Polish?"

"No, no, no!" Nancy cried. "Please try to understand. Mailman—letters—somebody steal them."

"Dere iss letter," the laundress said, pointing to Nancy's hands.

Nancy looked down and was surprised to see that the mysterious letter from England was still in her grasp.

"No, not this letter. Lots of letters. In a bag! Bad man steal!"

The woman looked at the excited girl with pity as if grieved that such a pretty young woman should be so utterly desperate.

"You come back odder time," she said with finality. "You go home, yes?"

The door was firmly closed in Nancy's face.

"Oh, what shall I do!" Nancy cried.

She walked to the curb and looked up and down the street. It was vacant, except for a small boy roller-skating on a driveway a hundred yards or so distant.

Toward him Nancy ran at top speed.

"Hello, Tommy, big boy," she hailed, recognizing the little fellow. "Did you see anyone acting suspiciously around here? The mailman's pouch with all the letters in it was just stolen from my porch."

"Golly, Miss Drew!" The boy's eyes were round with wonder. "Who did it?"

"Who did—goodness, that's what I'm trying to find out," Nancy cried. "Have you seen anyone go up our walk?"

"Only that man in the car," Tommy said.

"What man in a car?" Nancy demanded.

"Well, he didn't go up your walk in a car," the youngster said. "He left his car across from the Walker's. But he wasn't a burglar. He didn't have a mask on. He was a nice man, Miss Drew."

"What did he look like?"

"Well, nice."

"Oh, Tommy, don't say 'well' all the time. It's far from well. How was he dressed?"

The little boy pondered a moment.

"He had on a cap, a real light cap, and a

beautiful yellow overcoat, but his car was only an old tin thing."

"Which way did he go?" Nancy pressed him.

"Oh, down that way, I think."

"Thanks, Tommy! You have helped me a lot already!"

Determined that the robber should be swiftly brought to justice, Nancy ran back to the house. Ira Dixon still sat slumped against the porch pillar, while George and Bess hovered around trying to console him.

Hannah Gruen stood in the doorway, with Nancy's coat in her hands.

"You'll catch your death of cold out in just that thin dress," the housekeeper cried.

"Thanks, I didn't have time to think of the coat," Nancy said, thrusting her arms into the sleeves of the furred garment, and stuffing the still unopened letter into a pocket.

"Nancy is all business," George smiled. "Here a brand new mystery has walked right up to her front door. Don't worry, Mr. Dixon. Nancy has recovered more valuable stolen goods than just a lot of letters. They were probably mostly bills that nobody wanted, anyhow."

"No matter what they were," the mailman groaned, "it means my dishonorable discharge from the service, and I was so proud of a clear record."

"I have a description of a man who stopped

his car down the street a ways and who came up to our door," Nancy announced.

"Already?" Bess gasped. "Cheer up, Mr. Dixon, do! The robber is as good as caught."

Bess and George were not joking or exaggerating just to cheer the prostrated Dixon. They were confident that the thief was practically as good as captured, for they had seen Nancy distinguish herself time and again with her uncanny instinct for sleuthing.

Nancy always said she could not help being interested in mysteries, because her father, Carson Drew, famous as a criminal lawyer far beyond the boundaries of his home town, River Heights, or even the state, had to deal with mysteries as well as other kinds of cases in his practice.

Left motherless when a mere child, Nancy had developed into a self-reliant, keen-thinking girl, and although not yet of legal age her father often said she was a more helpful partner to him in his work than any man he could pick from the legal talent of the county.

At any rate, we have ourselves seen how Nancy established a reputation of her own in what came to be known to her friends as "The Secret of the Old Clock," which is the title of the first volume in this series.

After that it seemed as if persons had more trust in Nancy's ability than they had in professional detectives, and not without reason. A long list of the thrilling adventures which have so far been recorded has proved this.

After solving "The Secret of Red Gate Farm," Nancy found herself involved in combatting a scheming and fraudulent promoter who was swindling more than one trusting inventor out of the fruits of his toil. It was by means of "The Clue in the Diary" that Nancy solved the crook's secret, and incidentally became the friend of Ned Nickerson, a sophomore at Emerson University.

Ira Dixon was aware of Nancy's fame, and now he looked to the girl trustingly for help.

"The first thing to do is to report the theft," Nancy said briskly. "The postmaster will notify the United States Secret Service at once and they will get on the trail."

"I tremble to think of reporting this loss to the chief," Dixon said, as he arose shakingly to his feet. "What a confession to have to make!"

"The sooner it's over with the better," Nancy said. "Will you stay here until I come back, Bess—and you, George?"

"No, no. Run along, Nancy. We'll finish the cocoa and cakes and then take the bus home," the cousins replied.

"All right," Nancy agreed. "Come on, Mr.

Dixon. I'll drive you over to the post office."

The afternoon rush hour was just beginning as Nancy entered the business district of the city. Crowds were lined up at the trolley stops, buses were getting in each other's way, and private automobiles made the confusion worse.

Nancy's new car had all the latest devices, and its clever driver certainly utilized them, yet without taking undue chances. Dixon marveled audibly as Nancy took advantage of every opening, and when the traffic lights switched from red to green, had her car in motion before other autos in the line were started.

Nancy drove silently, her lips compressed. Her mind was busy with the mystery of the lost mail.

The post office was a large granite building, three stories high, topped with a tower. Nancy found a place to park nearby, then skillfully slipped her car into the space and leaped out.

"You lead the way, Mr. Dixon," she said. "I am going with you to help make explanations."

"Th—thanks, Miss Nancy," quavered the old man. "I'll be grateful for your support."

The unusual looking couple passed through the revolving doors of the post office, and Nancy followed the halting mailman to the elevator. On the top floor they stepped out opposite a door upon which was printed in gold letters:

OFFICE OF THE POSTMASTER

PRIVATE

Dixon hesitated, then slowly turned the knob. The door opened upon an anteroom where a clerk sat at a desk.

"Hello, Ira! How's tricks?"

"Hello, Joe. Is the chief in?"

"He's just getting ready to leave."

"I must see him."

The clerk arose and knocked at a door with a ground glass pane. A deep voice bade him enter, and a moment later the man emerged and with a jerk of his head indicated that Dixon was to go in. The old man walked slowly, his shoulders bowed. Nancy followed, her head held high.

The only occupant of the room was a tall, heavy-set man, who was putting on his overcoat. He looked at the girl in astonishment from under shaggy black brows.

"Mr. Cutter, this is Miss Drew," Dixon said. "I—I don't know how to explain it, but my mail pouch was stolen from her porch this afternoon."

"What!"

The postmaster's face turned crimson and

Nancy thought for the moment that he was going to burst a blood-vessel.

"Your pouch stolen—and the mail?"

"About twenty letters and some second and fourth class matter," Dixon admitted.

"How did that happen?" Cutter demanded, jerking off his coat and plumping himself into his desk chair.

"Perhaps I can explain," Nancy said, stepping forward. "It is all my fault, anyhow. Mr. Dixon came with our mail this afternoon. (Here Nancy's fingers closed upon the mysterious foreign letter in her pocket.)

"He always stops for a little chat, because we live near the end of his route. I coaxed him to step inside the door for a cup of hot cocoa, and in the moment his back was turned somebody snatched his pouch from where he had left it just outside the door."

"Great Heavens! Dixon, was there any registered matter or insured stuff in the bag?"

"Just the one registered letter Mrs. Sheets gets every week, Sir."

"Miss—Miss whatever your name is, this is a very grave matter," Cutter cried, pounding the top of his desk with a huge fist. "Of course, Dixon here will suffer for it. I suspend him at once. But you—you are the one to blame!"

CHAPTER III

A STORMY HALF HOUR

"I REALIZE that it was my fault," Nancy returned, without raising her voice, although her cheeks burned with an angry flush.

"I suppose you are awfully sorry it happened, and all that," sneered Jesse Cutter. "Well, young lady, I suppose you don't realize that this is a black mark on my record? In the long run it's I who's responsible for the lost mail!"

"Really, you don't have to shout at me," Nancy said. "I am not deaf, and I am aware of all you say. I came here to make what amends I could."

"Amends, bah! Seeing that the bag vanished from your home, you are not entirely clear of responsibility yourself," he growled.

"You don't mean to insinuate that I took the pouch, do you?" Nancy asked, stepping up to the desk and leveling her gaze at the irate postmaster.

"That's neither here nor there," that worthy responded. "Joe! Hey, Joe!"

The clerk opened the door with such celerity
it was evident that he had been standing with
an ear to the keyhole.

"Joe, get me the Chief of Police on the wire.
Then put through another call to the marshal's
office."

Cutter jerked a telephone toward him and
held the receiver to his ear, without relaxing
his baleful stare.

"Hello! Headquarters? You, Chief? Cutter at the P.O. speaking. Got a case for you.
Mail pouch stolen from a carrier on his route.
Send me the best detectives you have right
away."

He slammed the receiver down and jerked a
second telephone toward him.

"Hello!" he roared into the mouth-piece. "Is
that you, Brannigan? Oh, Berger? You'll
do. A bag of mail was stolen from a carrier
on his route this afternoon. Yes, the dumbbell
went into a house to call on a girl and left his
pouch out in the road. Hop around, will you?"

He shoved the instrument away from him
and turned snappily toward Dixon.

"You know this means your finish!" he
roared.

Dixon nodded, wordlessly. Nancy looked at
the faithful old carrier, tears of pity in her
eyes. Decades of faithful toil, a perfect record
maintained through difficulties at which she

could only guess, and then on the eve of honorable retirement, disgrace!

"Mr. Cutter," she said to the postmaster, "after all is said and done, Mr. Dixon feels much worse over this than you do. I don't see that your scolding and shouting help matters in the least. I came here to help. I have a brief description of a suspect, but we are wasting time now."

Cutter's eyes nearly popped out of his head.

"Of all the impudence in the world!" he roared. "You dare to tell me how to run my office and how to maintain discipline? Who are you, I'd like to know. Miss Wise Lady from Know-it-all, hey?"

Dixon put up an arm as if to ward off his superior's blistering words from his young friend, but Nancy was fully capable of taking her own part. She was not in the least ruffled by the postmaster's rudeness.

Waiting until he had finished, she merely asked:

"Are you interested in the description of the thief?"

"You can tell it to the Secret Service man," Cutter snarled. "Ah, here he is now. Come in, Berger."

Nancy turned to confront a most ordinary looking person, a man of medium height, with medium brown hair, a medium length nose—

medium in every respect, which made him a
very good Secret Service man indeed, for he
looked like anything but a detective.

"What's the fuss?" he asked quietly.

"This man here lost his mail pouch while
calling on this young lady during working
hours, that's what the fuss is about," Cutter
barked.

Nancy, with a scornful glance at the official,
told in as few words as possible the story of
the afternoon's mishap, and added the description of the suspected stranger as given her by
Tommy.

"That was good work," the Secret Service
man said. "All right, Cutter, I'm on my way."

"You know what to do," Cutter said.

As Berger left, two other men entered the
room. Through the open door Nancy caught
sight of a score of men in the blue-grey uniform of mail carriers, all crowding into the
anteroom to listen to the scandal.

"We're from Headquarters," one of the new-
comers announced.

"Oh, yes, boys. Come in."

Cutter repeated his boisterous and unfair
description of the theft.

"And is this the dame?" one of the detectives asked with a jerk of his thumb toward
Nancy.

"Please let me tell you what really happened," Nancy said, and again gave the story of the robbery in detail.

"We got your address, but what's your name?" the other plainclothesman asked, when she had finished.

"I am Nancy Drew."

The detectives looked at each other, and then at Cutter, who leaned back in his chair with a changed expression on his face.

"You mean—THE Nancy Drew?" he asked.

"I'm the only one by that name in town," she said simply.

Jesse Cutter leaned forward and there was a tone of respect in his voice when he spoke again. Carson Drew was a power in politics, and his daughter was not one to treat with disrespect.

"Why didn't you tell me who you were?" he asked, gently for him.

"Mr. Dixon introduced me by name when we came in," Nancy replied coldly.

"I—I didn't hear," Cutter said.

The plainclothesmen were also a little more courteous, but not more friendly. They had been twitted more than once by civilian acquaintances because of Nancy's solution of problems which had baffled the police, and now that they were face to face with the young woman, her youth and composure nettled them more than a little.

"No use running her in to Headquarters, then," said one to the other.

"Gosh, no!" replied his team-mate. "Come on, let's get on the job. Do you want this old bird run in, Chief?"

"No, he's under bond and Uncle Sam will keep an eye on him," Cutter said.

He turned toward Dixon again.

"You may go home and stay there until you are wanted, Dixon. I suppose you know better than to leave town until this is cleared up."

"Certainly, certainly," Ira replied, clenching his fists nervously. "I want this cleared up so my record won't be spoiled, of course. I'll do anything you say."

"And you, Miss Drew," Cutter rose and smiled, "of course you will forgive my little burst of temper. It upset me, the news you brought. We'll let bygones be bygones, and I thank you for your help in this matter."

Nancy pretended not to see his outstretched hand.

"Of course I intend to do all I can to help my old friend Mr. Dixon," she said sweetly. "Good afternoon, Mr. Cutter. If you will excuse Mr. Dixon, I'll drive him home."

"Certainly, certainly," said Cutter, staring at his still outstretched palm. Hastily he withdrew it and stuffed it into his pocket.

Nancy opened the door.

The anteroom and corridor were thronged with carriers and clerks, who hastily moved toward exits and stairs as Nancy emerged with Dixon.

All eyes were upon her, however, but with the composure of a queen Nancy walked through the curious throng to the waiting elevator. Then rose the voice of Cutter, shouting at the men to leave the office and be about their business.

"I—I'm obliged to you many times," Dixon said to Nancy. "I can never thank you enough for standing by me, Miss Nancy. I can't go with you now, though. Mr. Cutter was mistaken. I must stay and make out a report."

"Don't thank me," Nancy said, squeezing the old man's arm encouragingly. "I'll try to do something to really win your praise. Now tell me something. Where does your half-brother live and what does he look like?"

CHAPTER IV

NANCY'S SUSPECT

"You mean—Edgar?"

Ira Dixon looked at Nancy in bewilderment.

"Yes, the one who is after a part of your inheritance," Nancy nodded.

"Why, I—I don't know where he lives, to tell the truth," Dixon said. "Why?"

"Doesn't it occur to you that he might have taken your mail pouch for revenge?"

"That is a possibility," he said. "After all, there isn't a soul in the world with any grudge against me except Edgar."

Nancy said nothing, as Dixon paused. Then he went on:

"But no, Miss Nancy, I can't believe he would do such a thing just for spite. He knew how proud I was of my record. No, he wouldn't be so mean. He may be greedy, but not cruel."

"If you don't know where he lives it doesn't matter, then," Nancy replied, with a shrug of her shoulders. "However, I shall try my best to aid you and also get my father to help straighten matters out for you."

"Thank you a thousand times, Miss Nancy," cried Dixon, grasping one of the girl's hands in both his own. "You give me courage, you do indeed. I——"

The mailman's voice broke, and he turned his head. Nancy patted him on the shoulder and went out into the street.

"Oh, bother! It's dark," she exclaimed. "I thought I'd have a chance to read my letter from England in the car."

The swift autumnal twilight had set in, and Nancy switched on her parking lights to comply with the "sunset law." Although traffic was still thick in the heart of the city, Nancy threaded through it without difficulty and in a few minutes drew up in front of her home.

"Yoo hoo!" George hailed her from the porch. "We're still here!"

"Your father came in just as we were leaving so we told him all about the robbery," Bess explained when Nancy reached the porch. "We were just starting for the bus now."

"Then I'll drive you home," Nancy said promptly. "It will take less than half the time, and you can carry some of those apples with you. Mrs. Burd gave me a bushel when all I asked for was two quarts."

Nancy went into the kitchen and returned at once with four large paper bags heaped with apples, and a big squash.

Bess and George relieved her of the apples, while Nancy explained that neither she nor her father cared for squash and one of the other girls might as well make use of it.

"Not I, thanks just the same," George laughed. "Squash—ugh! I'd rather eat—cornstalks."

Bess Marvin, whose plump curves indicated a much heartier appetite than that of her cousin, put in a bid for the vegetable.

"I like it—squash pie, squash pudding, baked squash and buttered squash! Mmm! You don't know what's good."

"Let's go, then," Nancy cried. "And I'll tell you what happened at the post office as we're driving. Dad's locked himself up in his study, Hannah tells me, and said he wanted dinner late, so I have an hour yet."

In about twenty minutes Nancy drew up in front of George's home, a more modest dwelling than the Drew house. George jumped out, received her apples, and after exchanging farewells and plans for the next meeting of the three, left her friends.

Bess lived only two blocks farther on, and in no time at all Nancy was bidding goodnight to her second passenger.

"I'll drop around tomorrow if I have the chance," Bess said. "Whew, but it's getting cold and windy. Real football weather!"

"I haven't planned a thing for tomorrow,"
Nancy said. "Say, I'd better give you a hand
with this stuff. There is a hole in the bag of
apples and they might spill out. Here, you take
the squash."

The apple bag ripped as Nancy picked it up.
Hugging it to her chest, she scurried for the
Marvin door, but a pace from the front steps
the bag tore wide open from the weight of the
apples, and the crimson fruit went rolling in
all directions.

Bess dropped her squash, and the two girls,
with much laughter and scrambling under
bushes, retrieved the apples. It was quite dark
by now, and the brisk wind sent the last with-
ered leaves whirling from the trees.

"Br-r-r! That feels like winter," Nancy
cried, gathering up the corners of her coat and
making for the house with her recovered
apples.

Mrs. Marvin opened the door and then immediately ran for a dishpan to hold the fruit.

"Look out, Nancy," she said. "You are going to lose a letter from your pocket."

"Oh, my letter from England!" Nancy exclaimed, taking out the crisp envelope and con-
templating it again. She was half tempted to
ask permission to read it then and there.

"It's a curious thing," she laughed, "but this
is the first letter from England I ever got in

my life. I can't guess whom it is from. It's
addressed to 'Nancy S. Drew,' and I have no
middle name."

"Why don't you open it now, then?" Mrs.
Marvin suggested. "There is some printing
on the back."

"Oh, it's more fun speculating as to what is
inside," Nancy smiled, turning the letter over.
"Sure enough, there is a name on the back. I
hadn't looked. It says 'Chelsford, Lincoln,
Chelsford and Bates-Jones, Solicitors.' Oh,
that spoils my fun. I suppose it is someone
soliciting for charity."

Nancy stuffed the unopened letter back into
her pocket.

"I know," Bess laughed. "Nancy's detective instinct is aroused, and she is trying to
deduce what is in the letter without opening
it. Why don't you hold it to your forehead and
shut your eyes, Nancy, like the mind reader
we saw at Coster's Theater that time?"

Her chum laughed, too.

"Nancy has another real mystery," Bess said
to her mother.

"Indeed?" Mrs. Marvin exclaimed.

"I brought this one on myself," Nancy said
ruefully, buttoning up her coat. "Bess will
tell you all about it. I must hurry home to
dinner."

Nancy bade her friends goodnight and

stepped out into the darkness. The high wind was rattling the tree branches and whirling the fallen leaves about.

"What's that white thing being blown about in the air?" cried Bess from the doorway. "It isn't your letter, is it?"

Nancy, one foot on the running-board of her car, looked back to see a white object tumbling by, a dozen feet from the ground. Then she put a hand into her pocket. The letter was still there.

"It's nothing but a little piece of newspaper," she called to Bess.

As her chum closed the front door, Nancy gathered her coat tightly about her, stepped into the car, and turned on the motor.

She did not notice that the mysterious letter from England had been pushed from her pocket and had fluttered to the running-board, where a gust of wind had flattened it momentarily against the side of the moving car.

CHAPTER V

A Visitor

As soon as Nancy shifted to high gear she switched her lights from "parking" to "bright." When the car gathered speed Nancy noticed that the left headlight was flickering.

"Bother!" she exclaimed to herself. "That lamp is going to burn out in a second."

Instinctively she slowed down, whereupon the light burned brightly once more.

"Perhaps it is only loose," Nancy thought. "I'd better look at it."

She drew up to the curb. The wind, roaring out of the northwest, rushed down the street, sending a swirling mass of leaves and papers before it. Nancy felt something flat and hard strike one cheek, as she stepped out, and saw a white object fall to the roadway.

She stooped and picked it up.

"Gracious, it's my letter!" she said aloud. "Now, where in the world did it come from?"

Folding the stiff envelope twice Nancy stuffed it back into her pocket and put her gloves on top of it to hold it secure.

Examination of the headlight proved her surmise to be correct, that the bulb was only loose in its socket. With that little matter remedied Nancy started homeward again and reached her goal without further difficulty. She put the car in the garage beside her father's more expensive coupé, and entered the house through the rear door.

Hannah was leaning over the stove, ladling out soup.

"Dinner ready in five minutes," the faithful old housekeeper said.

"I'll be down as soon as I wash and run a comb through my hair," Nancy called over her shoulder. "And the air has given me an appetite like a pack of wolves."

Carson Drew was waiting behind his daughter's chair when Nancy, tidied and refreshed, entered the dining room. She greeted her parent with a kiss, her eyes shining with pride. Nancy was proud of her father; proud not only of his ability and accomplishments, but also of his distinguished and handsome appearance.

"George and Bess were telling me that old Dixon had an unfortunate experience here this afternoon," Mr. Drew said, as he ate his savory soup.

"Yes, I took him to the post office. The postmaster was very rude and loud, and said the robbery was really my fault," Nancy said.

"Cutter is a bumptious fellow," Mr. Drew commented. "Please pass me the salt, Nancy. What is your theory on the robbery?"

"I haven't made up my mind," Nancy replied. "I suspect Mr. Dixon's half-brother, who has been trying to get a part of the old man's little inheritance, of some spite work."

"Does Dixon agree with you there or haven't you mentioned it to him?" Mr. Drew asked.

"I did," Nancy said succinctly. "And he doesn't."

"Has it occurred to you that the robbery might have been committed to embarrass us?" Mr. Drew suggested. "It will look rather strange in certain newspapers that Miss Nancy Drew called the mailman into the house a few minutes for the first time of their long acquaintanceship, and then suddenly his pouch is stolen."

"I hadn't thought of that," Nancy admitted.

"I have just been appointed special State's Attorney to prosecute the Carvell Ring," Mr. Drew said. "You remember the river dredging scandal, don't you? The appointment was announced by the governor this morning. It may be that this robbery will prove an attempt to discredit me."

Nancy pondered this while Hannah changed the plates and brought in the roast.

"I don't know, Father," she said at last.

"It just doesn't seem like the sort of trick a political gang would commit. Mr. Dixon was near the end of his route. No one of any great importance lives beyond us. He turns down the next street and at the end of the block he winds up with the two or three houses in Wheelwright Alley—not more than a dozen houses in all.

"There would be no way of making it appear you were trying to intercept important mail, you see.

"I'm convinced that the robbery was to injure Dixon, and not you. There are dozens of ways for crooks to try to attack your legal reputation, but this is the only way Dixon could be harmed."

"A sound argument and good reasoning," smiled Nancy's father. "You'll be a lawyer some day and find yourself a Congresswoman, if you don't watch out."

Nancy laughed at the mental picture of herself in Washington.

"Speaking of lawyers, I got a letter from an English firm today," she said.

"An English firm? What did they have to say?"

"I haven't been able to find out," Nancy said.

"So they wrote you in a foreign language?" Mr. Drew laughed.

"No, no!" Nancy corrected him. "I just haven't had a chance to open the letter. A dozen times I've started to rip the envelope and something always turned up to prevent me. It is in my coat pocket. It has waited this long, so it can wait until after dinner."

"The letter was for you, you say, and not for me?" Mr. Drew inquired. "It was not from Bannister & McLean, by any chance?"

"No, it was from Somebody, Lincoln, Somebody & What's-his-name," Nancy smiled. "A great, long name I can't remember."

"Probably somebody has unearthed the fact that we are lineal descendants of William the Conqueror and you are being offered the crown of Great Britain for a price," Mr. Drew teased. "Well, never mind. How about another piece of this veal?"

"No, thanks, Dad," Nancy said. "But tell me this. Will they try to send Mr. Dixon to jail if the mail is not recovered?"

"I scarcely think so," Mr. Drew answered. "He will probably be dismissed from the service, and his pension forfeited."

"I think that is too bad," Nancy cried. "After all those years with a perfect record, too, for his work!"

"I feel sorry for the man," Mr. Drew said, "and I'll be glad to do what I can to help clear him. Tell him, if you see him again, to feel perfectly free to call upon me for any legal advice.''

"That's good of you," Nancy said. "I did not expect you would do less."

"And now, what's for dessert?"

"Apple-turnover, made from some fresh fruit from Red Gate Farm," Nancy announced. "George and Bess and I came back with the roadster loaded with delicious things! Tomorrow we'll have fresh pumpkin pie!"

Dessert and coffee finished, father and daughter left the table.

"I just want to glance over the evening papers, and then I'll have to lock myself in with the papers in the Carvell indictments," Mr. Drew said. "Will you excuse me, Nancy? You see very little of your father these days, but even so, think of him with kindness, won't you, dear?"

"Oh, if you'll just drop me a postcard from time to time," Nancy teased. "A view of the courthouse, maybe, or of the Lawyers' Building. And speaking of postcards makes me think of my letter again. This time I am going to open it and read it, even though there should be an earthquake, a flood, an attack by Indians and a broken leg!"

Nancy walked into the hall to the coat closet, and from her pocket withdrew the mysterious letter. She could not get her finger under the fiap, and the paper was of such excellent quality she could not tear open the envelope.

"I'll have to ask Dad for his knife," she thought, and approached her parent, who was half hidden behind the *Evening News-Banner.*

"I have the letter and I shan't put it down, but I can't open it," Nancy said. "May I have your knife, please?"

Without taking his eyes from the paper Mr. Drew plunged a hand into a trouser pocket, took out his knife and passed it to his daughter.

"You ought to see what the editor of this paper says about my appointment," he chuckled. "Let me read you a line or two. 'In appointing Carson Drew a special State's Attorney to prosecute the—' Hello! Somebody at the door?"

The front door-bell broke in with a sharp peal on Mr. Drew's reading.

"I'll see who it is," Nancy said, and still gripping letter and knife she ran to the hall.

First she switched on the lights which illuminated the porch, and then opened the door to admit the caller.

"Hello, Nancy Drew!"

"Why, Ned Nickerson, of all persons!" the girl cried. "Do come right in!"

The young man entered and removed his coat.

"Please go right into the living room,"

Nancy directed. "Dad, here's Ned Nickerson."

"How do you do!" Mr. Drew exclaimed in greeting.

"Good evening, Mr. Drew," the young man smiled, shaking hands vigorously with his host. "I just came into town from college to make some plans with Mother and Dad which concern Nancy, here, if you will consent."

Nancy's Mysterious Letter

CHAPTER VI

HEIRESS WANTED!

"THE Monday before Thanksgiving—next Monday, that is, will be Founders' Day at the University," Ned explained. "It's the day of our biggest football game of the year. We play State University, and the game ought to be a corker because both teams are unbeaten so far.

"I was wondering if Nancy would like to see the game, and if you will consent, Mr. Drew, Mother and Dad will take Nancy with them, and bring her back."

"Of course Nancy has my consent," Mr. Drew said without hesitation.

"Of course I'll love to go," Nancy cried. "I'm thrilled to think of it. Thank you, Ned!"

"No thanks at all," Ned protested. "I'm the one to be thanking you for being my guest."

"Let's see, you are on the team, aren't you?" Mr. Drew asked the youth.

"Yes," Ned replied. "It's my first year on the varsity, of course, because I'm only a sophomore. I'm just a substitute, but I've been in every game this season, so I have hopes of doing more than sit on the sidelines Monday."

"I think you are entirely too modest," Mr. Drew chuckled. "In going through the papers this evening—wait, let me see now—ah, here it is!"

Nancy's father opened one of the papers at the sports page, and while Nancy looked over his shoulder he read:

"Nickerson's Gifted Toe Threat to State! Drop-kicking Find of Coach Mullin's Eleven. Emerson Soph Has Not Missed Goal After Touchdown in Nine Tries This Season. Boots Four Field Goals."

"Oh, that's newspaper talk," Ned said, flushing. "I haven't started in the line-up of any game. I'm sub quarter-back, you see, and Farquhar, the regular, is the best quarter in the Middle West."

"I used to play myself," Mr. Drew said. "I played tackle, end and then left half-back for Hale twenty-two—no, twenty-three years ago. My, how time flies. It was a different game from the one you boys play now. No forward passes."

"It was a lot rougher, I guess," Ned commented.

"Rough?" Mr. Drew exclaimed. "Why, I remember against Kingston our full-back and captain, Graham—he's Graham of International

Zinc today—ran thirty yards for a touchdown with a broken collar bone.''

Ned and Mr. Drew plunged into a discussion of football too intricate for Nancy to follow.

She heard "flying wedge" and "five men on the line," "off-tackle" and "Minnesota shift," and decided it was as lucid to her as Mr. Drew's frequent mention of "Torts" and "nolle pros.," "status quo ante" and "post facto," Latin legal terms which tried her patience.

Nancy thereupon withdrew quietly to a far corner of the room, opened her father's pen-knife, and slit the tough paper of the envelope from England.

She unfolded the crackling, engraved sheet and eagerly read its typewritten message.

Her eyes grew wider and wider as she perused the letter, and as soon as she had read the last line she returned to the salutation and read it all over again.

Her re-reading completed, Nancy leaned back in her chair and stared into space.

By this time Ned and Mr. Drew were drawing diagrams of football formations on the margins of the newspapers.

"You see," Ned was explaining, "the left half runs to the right, with the full-back cutting ahead for interference, and the right half runs to the left. The quarter makes as if to pass the ball to the left half, and sprints ahead as if he had done so, but actually he gives the ball to the right half who throws a short pass over the line to the tackle or the end."

"That certainly is a puzzling play," Mr. Drew commented.

"If you think that's puzzling, listen to this," Nancy interrupted. "Your guess wasn't very far from the truth about this letter, Dad."

"Did you get into it at last?"

"Yes, and this is what it says," Nancy announced.

" 'My dear Miss Drew:
We are the legal representatives of the Estate of Jonathan Smith, late of Little Coddington, Midhampton, Berks., who died intestate on May 2, last. Mr. Smith had as only kin a sister, from whom he was estranged, a Mrs. Genevieve Smith Drew, who, we find, predeceased Mr. Smith by five years, leaving a daughter who is Mr. Smith's sole heir by law.

We have traced the daughter, Miss Nancy Smith Drew, to the United States, where our agents have been consulting directories and other sources for trace of her. You are the only Miss Nancy Drew so far discovered by them, and we beg of you to communicate with us.

If you happen to be the Miss Drew for

whom we are searching, will you be so good as to submit proofs of your identity, whereupon we shall be happy to make arrangements for your return to England.

After the inheritance and death rates are deducted the estate is of a size large enough to repay your interest.'

"And it is signed by a Mr. A. E. Lionel Bates-Jones," Nancy concluded. "What do you think of that?"

"Are—is it really you?" Ned asked.

"Of course not," Nancy laughed. "I was born right here in this town."

"What does it all mean?" Ned queried. "It is written in English, plainly enough, but I couldn't catch on to it all."

"Neither could I," Nancy confessed.

"In brief," Mr. Drew explained, "some wealthy man named Jonathan Smith died without leaving a will and his lawyers are trying to find his heirs. Smith had a sister with whom he had no communication, but she died before he did and her only child, this missing Nancy Drew, accordingly becomes heir to the fortune. They add that the fortune is of such size that even after the death and inheritance taxes, which are very large in England, are paid, there will be considerable wealth for the claimant."

"That settles it, then," Nancy laughed. "I am sailing on the next boat."

"And then?" her father asked.

"I'll use all the detective ability I inherited from you, Dad, to find out all about Jonathan even to his favorite dessert and favorite flower. Then I'll do the same by the late Mrs. Drew, and after buying a black veil I'll present myself as the missing heiress, produce my claims, take possession of the old moated castle and —presto! I'm rich!"

Ned looked a little worried. After all, he had known Nancy only a few months, and was not used to the little jokes she and her father played upon each other.

"They might trip you up, you know," he said anxiously. "It may be, that all the genuine Smiths of that branch have a peculiar birthmark or something."

"And that isn't all," laughed Mr. Drew. "You must remember, Nancy dear, you have two previous engagements which will prevent your departure for England.

"You have pledged yourself to attend a certain football game next Monday to cheer the future captain of the Emerson team to victory, and you have also nominated yourself a government agent to recover the stolen mail pouch!"

"That does rather complicate matters."

Nancy laughed. "Well, then, I'm afraid the great Smith fortune will just have to lie idle, drawing interest, until I have completed my other dates!"

Ned looked relieved.

"It would be an awfully risky thing to do, anyhow," he said with a shake of his head.

"Why, Ned, you goose," cried Nancy. "I was just pretending! If you thought for a minute that I would try to cheat that Nancy Smith Drew, I—why, I would—I wouldn't——"

"So was I play-acting," Ned grinned. "I was helping you play your little comedy. Now, if I thought for a minute you were going to England I'd turn you right over to Special State's Attorney Drew!"

So, with laughter all around, but a new mystery for Nancy to ponder over, goodnights were said all around.

CHAPTER VII

IRA DIXON'S APPEAL

AT THE door Ned paused.

"Do you know Helen Corning?" he asked.

"Yes, indeed I do," Nancy replied. "I haven't seen much of her lately, but we know each other well."

"She will be at the game, too," Ned said. "Buck Rodman, my roommate, has asked her. So you and they and my folks will all sit together, and Buck will guide you around."

"Splendid," Nancy said.

Nancy was sure she would have trouble going to sleep that night, as the day had produced so much that was exciting and affecting to the future.

Good health, however, triumphed and even as Nancy switched off her bed light, prepared to stare into the darkness for hours, her eyes closed and the next thing she knew Hannah was knocking at her door with the announcement that breakfast would be on the table in fifteen minutes.

Mr. Drew was so steeped in work that he

was reading a big, yellow, leather-bound law
book at the table, as Nancy entered the dining-
room.

"I shan't have a minute to spare all day,"
he said to his daughter. "I'm afraid you will
have to make your own plans for the time being, Nancy."

Nancy chipped the shell of her boiled egg
thoughtfully.

"Ira Dixon's troubles are on my mind most
of all," she said. "I don't know just what
course to take. Meanwhile I have decided to
write to the English lawyers and explain that
they are mistaken as to my identity."

"Then what?" asked her father.

"I'll offer to do what I can to find the missing heiress," Nancy announced.

"I'm afraid you are burdening yourself with
a lot of thankless tasks," Mr. Drew commented.

"Excellent advice from one who is so busy he
works at breakfast," Nancy replied dryly.

"The difference is that I get paid for my
work, and very well paid, too," Mr. Drew said.

"I get paid, too," Nancy said. "Of course,
I can't spend my pay, but it is a grand reward
to unravel the mysteries I encounter. If I
didn't, they would worry me."

"You are suffering from feminine curiosity
in an acute form," Mr. Drew laughed. "But
so long as it harms no one except those who

deserve to be discomfited, why, go to it Nancy.''

''I intend to,'' the girl said.

Immediately after breakfast Mr. Drew, his brief-case bulging, drove away to his office.

Nancy decided the first thing to do was to reply to the English lawyers. Accordingly she went into the library, took a sheet of her own stationery, and composed a letter to Messrs. Chelsford, Lincoln, Chelsford & Bates-Jones, explaining the mixed identities and offering to do all in her power to locate the lost heiress.

The letter finished, Nancy sealed it and decided to mail it at once.

''I'll pay the extra postage for the ship-to-shore airplane post,'' she thought. ''So the quicker I get this to the post office the better.''

She was just about to leave the house when the telephone recalled her. Ira Dixon was on the wire.

''I hate mightily to bother you, Miss Nancy, but I don't know where to turn for advice,'' he said, his voice thin and trembling over the wire. ''I hope you will find a minute to come to my home today. I'm quite ill from the shock of yesterday. May I hope to see you?''

''Why, of course you may!'' Nancy replied heartily. ''I was intending to drop in today, anyhow.''

''Bless you, Miss Nancy,'' Dixon said

warmly. "Just to talk with you a few minutes will make me feel well. I wanted to go see your father today, but I see by the morning paper he has a very important new case, so I don't want to bother him, even if I could manage to get to his office."

"Just stop worrying," the girl assured him.

Nancy's first stop was at the post office. She had passed the building thousands of times, had entered it often, but this morning the grim old place made her shudder a little as she recalled the scene within its walls the day before.

She half hoped, half feared that she might encounter Postmaster Cutter, but not one familiar face did Nancy see as she made her way to the airmail window. To the clerk in charge Nancy explained that she wanted the letter to reach its English destination as swiftly as possible.

"Let me see," said the man, consulting a big chart. "A ship—yes, the Consultania sails this afternoon. It is a five-day boat. I think your letter can catch it."

"Tell me how," Nancy begged. "It sounds impossible."

"We'll get your letter on the 10 A.M. air mail from here, which reaches New York—that is, the Newark Metropolitan Airport—at 4 P.M.," he explained to her. "It will be delivered to the Consultania by airplane at sea by 6 o'clock, if the weather is clear. There is a mail plane on board the ship and Friday morning it will be catapulted from the deck with the air mail, beating the ship to Southampton by a day. Your letter will be in the London post office Friday night.''

"Thank you so much," Nancy said, taking out her purse to pay for the postage. "I understood in a general way how the ship-to-shore air mail worked, but it is so much more understandable when one follows a specific letter across.''

"It won't be long before we'll have direct air mail at least daily," the clerk said, affixing stamps to the letter. "Then you can mail a letter here in the morning and it will be in England the next afternoon.''

Nancy's next destination was the home of Ira Dixon. The house was on one of the city's oldest streets, close to the river.

She had little trouble finding the place. Dixon's house proved to be a tiny, one-story cottage surrounded by a white-washed picket fence. It was a very old house, as the broad brick chimney and attached woodshed attested. A car was parked in front of the door.

As Nancy lifted her hand to the brass knocker the door was opened and a young man, carrying a black satchel, emerged.

"Oh—how do you do?" said he, cordially,

"Are you a friend or relative of Mr. Dixon?"

"An old friend," Nancy replied.

"I am Dr. Berger," the man explained. "Mr. Dixon is not well. The shock of the robbery—I suppose you know about that?—has prostrated him. I left him some stimulants and orders to stay in bed. You won't excite him, will you?"

"No, indeed," Nancy assured the physician. "I hope to make him more at ease."

The doctor bowed and walked toward his car, so Nancy entered the house without further ceremony.

The furnishings of the place were very plain. It was evidently the home of a bachelor, painstaking cleanliness unrelieved by those little touches which bespeak the feminine idea of comfort and decoration.

Nancy paused on the rag rug in the tiny living room, and called out:

"Mr. Dixon! This is Nancy Drew."

"Come right on in," Ira's voice replied weakly from the adjoining room.

Nancy entered to discover the old postman propped up on a couch, swathed in blankets. A chair was drawn up, and on it stood a bottle of medicine and a glass of water with a spoon.

"Find yourself a seat," Dixon smiled. "I'm sorry to be such a poor host."

"How are you going to manage about supplying food and heat?'' Nancy asked first of all.

"Mrs. MacGruder next door is being very kind to me," Dixon said. "It was she who insisted I have the doctor. She has promised to send me my meals until I am up and around again, and her oldest boy is tending my stove and feeding my guinea pigs."

"I must see them before I go," Nancy cried. "Where are they?"

"In the woodshed," Dixon explained. "Just go right through the kitchen. You'll like the ones with the curly hair. Those are Abyssinians."

"Have you heard from Mr. Cutter or from Edgar?" Nancy asked, as she settled herself in a chair.

"I haven't heard from a soul," replied Dixon.

"I suppose that Edgar will stay here to help you when he finds out you are sick," Nancy commented.

"Blood is thicker than water, and I am sure he will," Ira said with conviction. "Edgar is a wild boy, but I am sure his heart is in the right place."

"'A wild boy'?" Nancy repeated. "Is he much younger than you?"

"Oh, yes, he is thirty years younger than I," Ira said. "I could easily be his father, instead of his half-brother."

"Does he inherit the family's good looks?" asked Nancy with a merry smile, striving to amuse Dixon but at the same time to draw as much information from him as possible.

"Well, Edgar is a handsome lad," Ira admitted with pride in his voice. "And he always was a great fellow with the ladies. Miss Nancy, if you will go in the other room there you'll find an old album on the shelf under the table. There's a picture of Edgar in it that I'll show you."

Nancy found the old-fashioned plush album, and Ira turned its heavy pages. He selected a snapshot and gave it to the girl.

"That's a picture of Edgar taken when he was only eighteen, but he hasn't changed a bit," he explained. "He's of the dark, slender type that always looks young."

Nancy studied the picture with interest.

It showed a young man with sharp features, good-looking in a flashy sort of way. There was only the slightest resemblance to Ira. Edgar's black hair was slicked straight back, and grew lower on his forehead than did Ira's. His long, inquisitive nose and the rather close-set eyes reminded Nancy of a fox.

It was a face not at all distinguished, yet one not easily forgotten.

"He looks as if he would be an excellent dancer," Nancy said, returning the picture.

"I guess Dad and I spoiled him," Ira said, regarding the snapshot with fondness. "We gave him everything he wanted."

"What does he do for a living?" asked Nancy.

"Now that I don't know, either," Ira admitted. "He is always dressed very well. I sort of got the idea he was secretary to some big business man. But times are hard and his income is very much reduced, he told me. He planned to marry this winter, he said, but didn't think he could afford to right now."

"That's probably why he wanted a share of your money," commented Nancy.

"I guess so," Ira murmured. "I still think I ought to give him some, but it is such a small sum it won't do either of us much good if it is divided."

"It is a pity that you must consider dividing it with anyone," murmured the pretty girl thoughtfully as she considered the pattern of the rug beneath her feet. Somehow, its faded but delicate weaving reminded her of the fine old gentleman before her—he fitted so perfectly into the quiet surroundings. What a rude awakening would come to Ira if this stepbrother should prove to be a scoundrel! Nancy suddenly shook herself out of this depressing mood and with a thought of leaving, adjusted her scarf.

"I guess I had better run along," she said as she gathered her coat about her.

"No, no!" protested the postman, "do not hurry away. But there, I have no business burdening you with my troubles," he added painfully.

"Oh, do not worry, Mr. Dixon," Nancy answered quickly. "I just love mysteries and you have provided me with a real live one." She laughed confidently.

"I'm thankful," ruminated the letter-carrier, "that I gave you your mail before my bag was stolen. I believe you had a letter from England."

"I did," responded Nancy quickly. "Sometime when you are feeling better I will tell you all about its contents," she concluded gayly, trying to cheer the sad gentleman up a bit. "It was a great surprise."

Ira Dixon smiled upon the attractive, vivacious girl. He felt old, suddenly very, very old indeed, and the lines tightened about his mouth, as his worried mood returned. After a few moments of silence he said:

"Excuse me, I guess I'm not very entertaining, but I was thinking that if Mr. Cutter should come here, I'd get so nervous and shaky——"

Nancy interrupted him, saying soothingly, "Now, now, Mr. Dixon, don't cross that bridge yet. You just put your head back and rest."

She concluded that the old man needed sleep, and that she had stayed long enough.

"Is there anything I can bring you or do for you?" she asked, as she arose to go.

"I'm very well provided for, thank you again," Ira said with a wan smile. "I just wanted to be comforted a little, I guess. Does your father think they will put me in prison if the mail is not found?"

"He spoke of that," Nancy said. "No, there is no chance of that, Mr. Dixon."

"I—oh, there is someone at the door!"

"I'll answer it," Nancy said quickly, as the sound of the knocker reverberated through the little house.

She opened the door and was confronted by —Postmaster Cutter!

"Eh! You?" exclaimed the official.

"I just dropped in to see what I could do for Mr. Dixon," Nancy said. "He is quite ill from the shock. Please do not excite him. Those are the doctor's orders. I will tell him you are here."

She returned swiftly to the sick man's couch.

"Mr. Cutter is here," she whispered. "Do not let him excite you, and above all keep a stiff upper lip! We'll have this mystery solved before you know it."

"Oh dear! Oh dear!" groaned the shaking

postman. "I can't bear to have him berate me! He is so gruff!"

"Hush, Mr. Dixon, don't you dare let him see that you are nervous!" commanded the girl, trying to instill courage into the harassed letter-carrier. "Square your shoulders, be the fine gentleman that you are—and don't be afraid of any one, especially this pompous official! And I'll do all I can for you, and solve this mystery!"

As Nancy drove away, she wondered, however, just how she could make good her promise, but she was determined that she would not fail this faithful, grey-haired man. She must set to work at once!

CHAPTER VIII

The Missing Money

"OH, TOMMY!"

Nancy, returning from her visit to Ira Dixon, halted her smart little maroon roadster a few rods from her home.

The little boy who had seen the man she suspected of stealing the pouch was playing on his lawn.

"Hello, Nancy!" cried the child, running toward her.

"Tommy, have you seen anything of the man in the yellow overcoat?"

"Not again," said the boy, shaking his head.

"Tell me, did he have a long pointed nose?" quizzed Nancy.

"Like a elefunt's?" Tommy demanded.

"Oh, no! Just a regular nose, but sharper and longer than most men's," Nancy laughed.

"I don't know," Tommy replied. "He looked nice. But his car was no good. Old tin one, that's what."

"You are sure you didn't see him come back to the car with a mailman's bag?"

Tommy shook his head.

"Smoke was coming out of his car," he said. "It went 'chuff! chuff!' "

Nancy knew there was no use in hoping that Tommy could remember every detail of the stranger's actions. Evidently the yellow overcoat and the steaming car had made the greatest impression on the child.

It seemed to be almost as hopeless a quest as the English lawyers' search for Nancy Smith Drew.

Nancy drove to her home and parked the car at the curb. Hannah greeted her with the announcement that she would have luncheon ready in just five minutes.

"I didn't know for sure when you would be back," she said, "so I made some bouillon and I have cheese sandwiches all ready to toast."

"That sounds perfect to me," Nancy said. "Put lots of paprika on the toasted cheese."

Steps on the porch attracted her attention to the front door, which opened to admit Bess Marvin.

"Just in time for luncheon! I'm so glad I won't have to eat alone," Nancy cried.

"I had a sandwich and malted milk at Grey's," Bess said. "But I'll join you in some dessert."

"Oh, and a cup of bouillon, too," Nancy urged. "Hannah always makes enough for a regiment, and she has the most delicious trick of putting a speck of nutmeg in chicken bouillon—yum!''

''I can't resist, even if I gain another pound,'' Bess laughed. ''Lead the way.''

Scarcely had the girls entered the dining room when the doorbell pealed.

''Oh, dear, who can that be?'' Nancy sighed.

''I'll answer it,'' Hannah said, putting down the cups of broth.

To the ears of Bess and Nancy there presently came high-pitched voices.

''I tell you Miss Drew is just sitting down to lunch,'' Hannah shouted.

''And I tell you Miss Drew will be sitting in a cell in prison eatin' bread and water, so she will,'' a strange, high voice replied.

''What in the world—'' gasped Nancy, looking at Bess with apprehension.

''You can't come in!'' Hannah was heard to cry.

''Can't, hey? Well, I'm in, ain't I?''

Nancy rose from the table.

''I'd better go settle this,'' she said. ''Go ahead and eat, Bess. I'll be right back.''

In the front hall Nancy saw an irate Hannah holding the door ajar, confronting an equally angry, strange woman, who stood with hands on hips. She was slovenly dressed, with wrinkled stockings and scuffed shoes run over at the heels. A worn-looking short jacket of some cheap fur was pulled on over a faded gingham house dress, and her hair hung in loops over her ears.

"You're the lady I'm looking for, I guess," shrilled the woman as Nancy came into view.

"I am Nancy Drew," said the girl quietly.

"I know you are Nancy Drew," mimicked the stranger. "I've seen you go flibberty-jibbet in your auto many a time. When I was a girl, girls stayed home and learned to cook and sew and mind their own business, not to go gallivantin' around in swell autos and waited on hand and foot. I declare I don't know what the world is coming to."

"If you have come here to lecture me, would you mind waiting until I have finished my luncheon?" Nancy asked.

"Don't be pert with your elders, Miss," the woman snapped. "I didn't come here to lecture you. I came here to get my rights, that's all. And get 'em I will, or you'll suffer for it."

At this juncture Bess entered the hall and took her stand beside Nancy.

"Why don't you call the police?" she asked her chum.

"Call the police indeed!" retorted the woman. "It's me that ought to call in the cops!"

"Perhaps if you would tell us who you are

and what you want," Nancy said, "we might get somewhere."

"Sheets is the name, Mrs. Maude Sheets to you," the woman snapped. "I'm Sailor Joe Sheets's wife, which is my bad luck, him forever traipsin' off to all corners of the world leaving me to get along the best I can."

"All right, Mrs. Sheets," Nancy interrupted. "Now what is your grievance?"

"Grievance enough, I'll say," Mrs. Sheets shrilled. "Joe's sister, with all the money in the world and her not turning a finger but the money just pouring in because her husband invented some sort of mess that takes stains out of cloth, is condescendin' enough to send me ten dollars a week, if you please. And where is it this week, I ask you?"

"I'll bite," Bess said. "Where is it?"

"Ask that snippety-uppity Nancy Drew," Mrs. Sheets cried. "It was in the mail bag that vanished so mysteriously from this house."

"You have no right accusing me," Nancy said with spirit. "I've been working every minute since the unfortunate robbery to locate the bag!"

"Oh, dear me! How perfectly awfully too bad, I must say," Mrs. Sheets sneered. "I suppose you are close to a nervous breakdown from the strain of working so hard!"

"If you don't keep a civil tongue in your

head, Missus, I'll get the cops myself, so I will," Hannah fumed. "Or I'll lay the broad side of my broom against that impudent face of yours!"

Mrs. Sheets was taken aback for the moment at hearing someone reply to her in her own language.

"Hannah," said Nancy somewhat sharply, "go see about luncheon. I'll attend to this woman."

"Oh, hitey-titey!" crowed Mrs. Sheets, her courage renewed with her most able opponent sent off the field. "Quite the lady boss, just like all the Nancy Drews!"

"What do you mean, 'like all the Nancy Drews'?" Nancy demanded. "Have you known many of them?"

"Have I known many of them? Thank goodness, no!" Mrs. Sheets said, casting her hands aloft. "Just you and the other one, and you are both cut out of the same cloth, I'll say! Uppity and quite the grand ladies, and forever cheating poor working folks out of ten dollars!"

"Listen here, Mrs. Sheets, I did not take your ten dollars from the letter, and I could have you arrested for accusing me," Nancy said, taking a step forward.

"I suppose you can take advantage of all the twists in the law, being a smart lawyer's girl," Mrs. Sheets replied, undaunted.

"However," continued Nancy, ignoring the remark, "I'll personally make up the ten dollars you lost. I shall bring it to your house this afternoon."

Mrs. Sheets relaxed, her brows knit.

"Well, why didn't you say so in the first place?" was all she could think of to reply.

"Why didn't you say you were suffering because of the lost ten dollars in the first place, instead of making such a scene?"

"Well, I guess it worked, didn't it? I've got my ten dollars back, haven't I?" the coarse woman sneered.

"Not because I ever had it, though," Nancy said. "And now tell me something about this other Nancy Drew."

"Maybe I will when I get my ten dollars," retorted Mrs. Sheets.

"Don't give her the money until she tells you what you want to know," Bess suggested, although somewhat mystified at her chum's curiosity concerning the identical names.

"Is that so?" Mrs. Sheets cried. "I guess I'm not peddling information. I have a right to my ten dollars, without no ifs or buts!"

Hannah poked her face around the kitchen door at this juncture.

"The toasted cheese is like celluloid and the broth is stone cold," she announced.

"Then please excuse me, Mrs. Sheets, while

I go on with my luncheon," Nancy said courteously. "I promise you I'll bring the ten dollars to your home myself this afternoon."

"That's how it is with young girls these
days," Mrs. Sheets grumbled. "What's ten
dollars to them? Nothing. I'll bet your poor
father has to sweat to keep you decked out in
clothes and cars so you can hop around stickin'
your nose in other folks's affairs. When I was
a girl——"

To the intense relief of everybody except
Mrs. Sheets, the telephone rang just then.

CHAPTER IX

Two Slender Clues

Hannah answered the telephone, while Nancy held the door open for the wordy Mrs. Sheets.

"You needn't hustle me out, now," that woman continued to sputter. "Certainly the young folks of today isn't taught no manners at all. When I was a girl we was taught to know our places. I——"

"There's a very important call for Miss Drew," Hannah announced grandly. "Terribly important and terribly confidential."

"Excuse me, then," Nancy said, and turned from the door to answer the telephone.

Bess saw with considerable satisfaction how Hannah gave Mrs. Sheets a far from gentle shove, and shut the door, with what was close to a slam, in the woman's face.

"How you can keep your temper is beyond me," Hannah muttered, as much to herself as to Nancy. "Now I'll warm the soup and make some more toast."

The housekeeper stalked grandly from the

hall, conscious that she had routed the enemy.

Meanwhile Nancy, her ear to the receiver, was listening to a recital which made her heart beat faster.

"This is Ira Dixon, Miss Nancy. I thought I'd call you up. Edgar was just in to see me. He came in his car, he said, as soon as he read in the papers about the robbery."

"Yes, yes," Nancy cried. "Go on!"

"Miss Nancy, that boy had nothing to do with my hard luck, I'm sure of that," the postman continued. "Why, he was as sympathetic as you are yourself, and he tried to get me to give him some of my money to hire private detectives. If I had my inheritance in hand I'd have done it, but I couldn't put my hands on one hundred dollars to save my life!"

"Did he ask you to give him money to hire a detective?" Nancy asked. "Or did he suggest you hire one yourself?"

"I can't leave my room, you know," Ira replied. "Edgar was going to take care of all the details himself, he said."

Nancy had her own private idea just how much detective hire Ira would have got for his money, but she said nothing.

"So you see, your suspicions were all wrong," Ira continued.

"Did Edgar say where he was stopping?" Nancy asked.

"Yes, there is no secret about that," Ira went on eagerly. "He's boarding up in Stafford. He even gave me the address. I have it written down here—wait a minute——

"Hello? Here it is! He boards with a family named Hemmer in Harrison Street!"

"Well, that certainly seems to clear Edgar," Nancy said.

"I knew all along the lad wasn't bad," Ira said triumphantly. "He's my father's son, after all. He couldn't be a crook."

"Don't excite yourself, now," Nancy cautioned. "And I'll be around to see you the first chance I have. I didn't get a chance to look at the guinea pigs on account of Mr. Cutter arriving. What did he want, by the way?"

"He just asked me a lot of questions," Ira said. "Where and how and why—you know."

"Then goodbye until the next time, Mr. Dixon," Nancy said, catching sight of Hannah making despairing gestures in the dining room.

"Goodbye, Miss Nancy! Thank you for being good to an old man," Dixon said.

Nancy hung up the receiver.

"And now I hope we can eat without further interruption," she said, seating herself at the table and starting on her bouillon with vigor.

"I'm so weak I haven't strength to bite," Bess declared. "That terrible Sheets woman. Nancy, how could you keep your temper?"

"What good would getting angry have done?" Nancy asked. "And this way, I have a new clue."

"A clue to what? The missing mail pouch?" Bess asked incredulously.

"No, another mystery," Nancy said.

"Another! Gracious, Nancy, are mysteries getting so commonplace you must have two on the string at once?"

"Both of these came to me uninvited," Nancy smiled, munching her toasted cheese sandwich.

She told Bess of the contents of her letter from England, and how she had hurried a reply, assuring the lawyers that she would help them find the missing heiress.

"I should have a better chance than anybody else in discovering the other Nancy Drew," she explained. "If anybody who ever heard of the other Nancy were to meet me, the similarity in names would probably be mentioned right away."

"Oh, and Mrs. Sheets did mention another Nancy Drew!" cried Bess.

"That's just it, you see," Nancy laughed. "I found a clue by keeping the reins tight on my temper. I don't pretend for a minute that the woman didn't make me furiously angry, though."

"I think I should have pulled her hair,"

Bess confessed. "The nervy old thing! She certainly has no kind thoughts about modern young people, has she?"

"Oh, well, remember that couple at Red Gate Farm last summer?" Nancy smiled reminiscently. "They thought the world ought to come to an end because young folks didn't know their places any more. But they sang a different tune after the Sheet-and-Pillowcase Club was rounded up and put in jail."

"I'll never forget that Black Snake Colony," Bess declared fervently, "especially after we joined it without invitation!"

"Aside from all that, just imagine, Bess, I'm going to the big game Monday!" Nancy said.

"You mean the Emerson-State U game?" Bess cried. "Oh, how I envy you. I suppose Ned Nickerson asked you?"

"Yes," Nancy confessed. "He came last night and asked Dad if I might go up with his parents. After the game there are to be theatricals—The Merchant of Venice is going to be given by the college dramatic society."

"And I suppose Ned, besides being quarterback on the team, will play the part of Portia?"

"No, you old silly! Imagine a six-foot Portia with a bass voice! Ned is in the play but his part is not important," Nancy replied. "I think he said he was going to be 'shouts and murmurs off stage'."

The girls brought their luncheon to a merry conclusion.

"I must hurry to the bank to draw ten dollars for Mrs. Sheets," Nancy said. "Want to ride along?"

"Indeed," Bess agreed, "all I came for was to get the latest inside information on the robbery, and what entertainment I got instead!"

"It takes all sorts of people to make a world, it's said," remarked Nancy philosophically. "I never could understand, though, why it was necessary to have Edgar Dixons and Mrs. Sheetses and such people. It would be a better world without them."

"Then what would you do for mysteries, pray?" Bess laughed. "You would have to go to Mars or some other planet."

"Yes, and what would my father do for a living?" Nancy agreed. "I guess the queer folks and the bad ones both have their purposes but I'd rather have Dad a—oh, even a mailman like Ira Dixon—if everybody in the world were as good and kind as he."

"You can't make the world over, Nancy dear," Bess counseled. "So let's go to the bank for the money, or you won't be able to keep your promise. On the way down you can tell me all about the latest developments in the great United States Mail Robbery!"

"You are right, Bess," Nancy cried, throwing on her exquisitely furred coat. "Let's go!"

Bess took her place beside Nancy in the waiting roadster, and settled herself under the rug, as Nancy took the wheel.

"There aren't any good developments in the case. I went to see Mr. Dixon this morning, but——"

"That little boy seems to want to speak to you," Bess interrupted. "He's running after us and waving."

Nancy put on the brakes and looked around.

Little Tommy was racing down the street as fast as his chubby legs could carry him.

"I saw him!" he shouted. "I saw him!"

CHAPTER X

The Scolding

"I saw the bad man!" Tommy announced triumphantly from across the street.

"You darling!" Nancy said, climbing out of the car and hurrying across to the lad. "Tell me all about it."

"I was playing on the lawn again," Tommy said gravely. "I was playing I was a steamboat, like this, 'Choo! Choo! Choo! Toot toot!'"

"A lovely game," Nancy said hurriedly. "I have often played it myself, so don't tell me now. What about the man?"

"He drove past here real fast, going that way," Tommy said, pointing away from town. "He had the same yellow coat on, and the gray hat, and his auto made the same smoke."

"When was this, Tommy?" Nancy asked, holding out a bar of milk chocolate she had providentially found in a pocket. "What time was it?"

"Oh, about eleventeen," Tommy said gravely. "Is that my chocolate?"

Nancy realized Tommy was too small to tell time or to have any idea of it. She gave him the candy and patted the boy on his head.

"You are a fine little detective, Tommy," she said.

"Do you think I can have a badge?" the boy asked, unwrapping the chocolate bar.

"I'll see that you get one," Nancy promised.

She returned to her car thoughtfully. Edgar had been to town to see his half-brother. The car with the flashily dressed suspect had been going westward, which was the general direction for Stafford. Was it more than a coincidence?

Nancy concentrated on telling Bess about her visit to Dixon's house, relating in detail what had happened there and describing the furniture minutely. She did not want to expound her theories, even to her closest friend.

At last the bank was reached. A glance at the clock in the post office tower showed Nancy she had but two or three minutes before closing time to reach the teller's window.

"I'll be right back," she said to Bess, as she jumped from the car and ran toward the building.

The doors were of the sort that swung in either direction, made of metal with heavy plate-glass panes guarded from breakage by a heavy brass grill. The gloom within the bank and the bright light of the lowering sun outside made the glass in the doors reflect like mirrors.

Nancy saw herself in the pane as she shoved the door ajar, and not the person who was at the moment directly behind it.

"Oof! Ouch!" bellowed a voice. "Can't you see where you are going?"

She had shoved the door right into a stout man who had lost his balance and also a handful of papers as a result of the collision.

"Oh, I'm very sorry," Nancy cried sincerely. "I couldn't see through the door. The light made a mirror of it, and all I could see was the reflection of the street and myself."

As she spoke she stooped to help retrieve the scattered papers.

"That's just it, you were so busy admiring yourself you couldn't see me," growled the man. "I declare, young people these days are the most selfish, careless lot with no consideration for their elders at all."

The man and Nancy rose simultaneously, and as the girl held out the papers she had picked up she found herself staring into the countenance of none other than Jesse Cutter, the postmaster!

"You," the man exclaimed.

"Oh, Mr. Cutter, I'm really sorry I bumped into you," Nancy cried. "But I was in such a hurry——"

"I'll certainly agree you were in a hurry," scolded the official. "Now in my day young women didn't go flying around like—like wild turkeys. A woman's place is in the home, say I, and that goes for young ones who ought to be studying the business end of a broom or a darning needle instead of getting into trouble all the time."

Nancy thought that two doses of this sort of advice in one afternoon was all she could stand.

"Have you made any progress in finding the thief who took Mr. Dixon's pouch?" she asked pleasantly, to change the subject.

"No," he said curtly. "I still hold you morally responsible for the theft, young lady, even if you are Carson Drew's daughter. Now, when I was young, girls didn't go around inviting men below their station in life to come into their homes. That's the reason we have so much lawlessness these days. The young people aren't brought up right. They have no discipline at all. They think they know more than their elders, they do. They——"

" 'Scuze me, sah, but de bank am closin'," a colored porter interrupted, tipping his hat respectfully. "Ah jest natcherly got to shet de do'."

"Oh, not yet!" Nancy cried, darting into the building. She hurried to the window marked "Paying Teller."

"May I have a counter check, please?" she panted. "I know I'm late, but I must draw ten dollars."

The teller was a little cross as he handed Nancy a pink blank.

"Excuse me, Miss," he said, "but if you hadn't spent so much time in the lobby gossiping you could have spared me from working over-time."

Nancy felt that the whole world was unusually full of cross people this afternoon.

She made out the check and presented it with her pass-book.

"How'll you have it?" the clerk asked. "All in ones, or five twos or two fives, or how?"

"Just a single bill if it is convenient," Nancy said.

The teller handed her a crisp, new ten-dollar bill and slammed the wicket shut.

Nancy tucked the money into her purse and walked to the door, which the colored porter unlocked for her under the watchful gaze of two armed guards.

Bess was no longer in the runabout. Nancy saw a scrap of paper tucked beneath the gas lever on the wheel, and found it to be a note from Bess saying she had seen her father passing and had decided to complete her trip home with him.

"Good! That will give me time to go straight

to Sailor Joe's wife with the money," Nancy said, as she headed her car into the stream of traffic and swung around the block for the errand, which though a dreaded one was also an eagerly anticipated one.

"I hate to face that woman again, and yet I am sure she has a clue to the other Nancy Drew," she thought.

CHAPTER XI

At Sailor Joe's

As Nancy drove, her mind was revolving about the mysteries confronting her; yet she was constantly alert to all the perils and confusions of traffic, for she was instinctively a good driver, shifting and braking almost automatically.

"What a relief it will be to get up to Emerson and forget all about this for a few days," the girl said to herself.

"I'll have to do some shopping before I go, though. I'll wear my raccoon coat to the game, but I ought to have a hat in the Emerson colors. Orange and violet—hm! Perhaps one of those snappy new sport ones in violet with an orange feather. My lavender evening dress with the —no, I'll wear the deep yellow one with a corsage of violets. I'll have to get some new slippers to go with it, though."

Carson Drew gave his daughter a generous clothing allowance with the understanding that she could spend it as she pleased, but could not exceed the stipulated budget. If she wanted to splurge the whole amount for an extravagant fur coat, all right. But then, she would have to make all her dresses, frocks, suits and shoes, her stockings, handkerchiefs, underwear and powder do for the year.

Nancy, however, was a wise buyer. Her premature training as the lady of the house had taught her to know good values as well as to use common-sense in buying. There was not a year in the three during which she had enjoyed the allowance but that showed a surplus.

Nancy drove past her house, turned the next corner, and headed her car into the narrow, cobbled confines of Wheelwright Alley, where Sailor Joe lived when he was not sailing on some ship.

The bell knob on the cottage door was brightly polished—a sure sign, although Nancy did not know it—that Sailor Joe was home for the time being. Mrs. Sheets did not otherwise bother with such useless labors.

In answer to the bell the door was opened by the old salt himself.

"Howdy do?" he smiled affably. "We don't want to subscribe to no magazines, thank'ee."

"I'm not selling anything," Nancy laughed. "I came to see Mrs. Sheets."

"Well, she h'isted anchor here about an hour ago," Joe said. "I expect she's just rowed around to the chandler's for some supplies, and, most likely, she'll be back by eight bells."

"You mean eight o'clock?" Nancy asked in dismay.

"No, no! Eight bells in the first dog watch," Joe replied seriously. "That's, let me see, now—4 o'clock."

"Oh, then she will be back very soon," Nancy said, glancing at her wrist watch. "May I wait?"

"Heave your anchor, lass!" boomed the sailor. "Here, come into the pilot house!"

He led Nancy into the sitting room. It was papered in red, and furnished in a cheap style —oak mission furniture with imitation leather upholstery. On the walls were pictures of ships, a broken but highly polished sextant, a savage-looking spear, the vicious weapon of a sawfish, and a large dried starfish.

Nancy seated herself on the uncomfortable divan.

"Sailing all over the world, you must have seen many interesting things," she said.

"Ah, and so I have," Sailor Joe grinned, settling himself to spin a yarn. "Why, I mind the time—it was my first voyage to the South Seas, back in '84, it was—or was it '85? Well, no matter. I had shore-leave at Melbourne and I spent it as sailors will, you know, and when I wakes up next mornin' with a splittin' head-ache I sees as I ain't in my hammock on the *Mary K. Venner*, but on a pile of burlap in a strange craft. I was shanghaied!

"Well, to make a long story short, I was on a New Guinea pearler! The joke of it was, I couldn't even swim! Was that skipper mad!"

Nancy failed to see the joke which made Joe rock with laughter and slap his knees with great, calloused, tattooed hands.

"I remembered—ha-ha ho-ho!—I remembered tellin' a purser I met on shore I was willin' to do pearl divin'. Pearl divin' is what common sailors call washin' dishes. An' that purser thought I was a diver and shanghaied me to actcherly go over the side of the ship for pearl shell! Ho ho ho!"

Nancy now saw the humor of the sailor's adventure, but she had not come to the house for entertainment.

"How long have you lived here?" she asked.

"Maybe a year, maybe two," Joe said. "My old woman moved out here so's I'd be far from the sea, and maybe stay home. But I could smell salt water if I was in the middle of a desert, as I was once. It was back in '92, or was it in '93——?"

Nancy interrupted swiftly.

"Did you ever know a young woman named Nancy Drew?" she asked.

"Nancy Drew? Well, I'll say I did, and a trim little figure-head she was, and as neat as an admiral's cutter. Did you know her?"

Nancy shook her head.

"I'm trying to locate a Nancy Smith Drew who is wanted in England," she explained.

Sailor Joe bristled.

"Wanted in England, is she? And for what? That girl never did a wrong thing in her life."

"Oh, she isn't wanted by the authorities," Nancy hastened to explain. "A relative died and she was left some money."

"Aha! That's a jib of another cut," Joe grinned. "Yes, she used to room with the missus in New York. That was before we came here. On West 23rd Street, that was. My wife kept a roomin' house, then. Nancy Drew. Well, well!

"I'm glad she come into some money, for she was hard up, that she was. Studyin' for the stage, and a fine figure of an actress she'd have made. Tall and beautiful, with a fine deep voice on her besides. But she couldn't get to sign with any theater, and at last she left us to go to some beach with a family as a gov'ness."

Nancy was wildly elated.

It was all she could do to keep from shouting "hurrah!"

"When was this?" she asked excitedly.

"Oh, that was maybe ten—no, not that. Let me see, now. I remember I brought her back a souvenir and she was gone when I docked.

What did I bring her, then? I remember, it was a little monkey!

"Monkey—monkey. I got the monkey from a Portugee. I've got it! In Brazil! And I made the v'yage to Rio in—why, it's just eight years next Spring that she left us."

Eight years ago! Nancy's heart sank.

"Do you remember the name of the family she went with?" she pressed.

Sailor Joe pursed his lips and frowned.

"English folks, I think. Name of Washington, or was it Huckleberry? Something like that. I gave the monkey to a man in exchange for a pair o' boots."

Nancy felt that her quest had failed. She could see no similarity in the names Washington and Huckleberry, and Joe was evidently more familiar with the fate of his monkey than with that of the English girl.

"Ahoy! There's the missus," Joe exclaimed. "I know her step on the quarter-deck!"

He jumped to his feet and opened the door to admit Mrs. Sheets, still in the garb Nancy had seen her in before. Her arms were loaded with bundles.

"Brisket corned beef is what you'll get for supper, because it's the cheapest cut in the market," the woman announced to her husband.

"Salt horse again!" exclaimed the sailor. "Well, never mind, we've got company."

Mrs. Sheets turned upon Nancy, who rose with a smile.

"Humpf! It's you, is it?" Mrs. Sheets sniffed. Without another word she passed through the room to the rear of the house, and it was some minutes before she returned, divested of coat and hat.

"Did you bring the money?" she snapped.

"Hey, what's all this palaverin' about?" Joe cried.

"This is the young lady at whose house the letter from your sister disappeared," Mrs. Sheets explained. "I went around there this noon and her royal highness here at last agreed to make up what we lost."

Joe looked from his wife to Nancy in bewilderment.

"But this missy didn't steal the money, did she?" he demanded.

"I'm asking no questions," Mrs. Sheets said stiffly. "No questions asked, and no reward given. All I want is our money."

"I didn't steal the money, Mr. Sheets," Nancy smiled. "I don't have to steal, I assure you. But the money was stolen, together with the other mail, from my house, so I think it is only right that I should make amends."

"Not even a sea-lawyer would agree to that, or I'll be keel-hauled," Joe roared.

"I propose to pay the money just the same."

Nancy said firmly. "I will not have Mrs. Sheets suspecting me of robbing her."

"Never mind the tall talk," Mrs. Sheets interrupted. "Let's see the color of your money."

"Just a moment," Nancy said, summoning all her self-composure. "I was talking with your husband about the other Nancy Drew. He painted an altogether different picture of her than you did, Mrs. Sheets. And he said that she eventually left your place to become a governess."

"What about it?" Mrs. Sheets asked tartly.

"I wish you would try to recall the name of the family to whom she went," Nancy said.

"I don't remember," snapped Mrs. Sheets.

"Come on, now, skipper," Joe said. "Sure you can remember. Wasn't it Washington?"

"No, it was not."

"Then Huckleberry. Or something between the two."

"It certainly was not Huckleberry," Mrs. Sheets snapped. "I never heard no such name."

"I'll think of it," Joe said, cudgeling his forehead. "Huckleton—no. Maybe Washberry? Not that."

"I'll trouble you for my money, Miss," the woman said to Nancy.

Nancy took the bill from her purse, hoping

that the sight of it would loosen Mrs. Sheets's tongue.

"Hey, avast there!" Joe cried. "Stow that money, Miss. We don't want it."

"What do you know about money?" snapped Mrs. Sheets, reaching past her husband and snatching the bill from Nancy's grasp.

"I didn't believe you'd bring it," she said in a less severe voice. "But now I guess there's no loss in telling you where the other Nancy Drew might be. She went with a family named Hutchinson—Thomas Hutchinson. I forwarded enough mail to her, to remember that. Thomas Hutchinson, at the Breakers Hotel on Cape Cod."

"Thank you," Nancy said heartily. "That was information worth any trouble to get."

She walked to the door on winged feet.

CHAPTER XII

Inspiration

NANCY left Sailor Joe's cottage in high spirits. She was convinced that it would not be difficult now to locate the English Nancy.

"Even if there are dozens of Thomas Hutchinsons in New York, it is just a matter of time until I find the right one," she said to herself, as she drove out of the alley.

Nancy laid her plans as she drove the short distance to her home, and by the time she had the car in the garage and her hat and coat off, a tentative course of action had been laid.

"I'll borrow a New York telephone directory from the library, or the 'phone company," she planned. "Then I'll copy the names and addresses of all the Thomas Hutchinsons and write to each one."

On the hall table Nancy found the day's mail and picked up the batch to assort in the living room. All of Mr. Drew's business correspondence was directed to his office, and Nancy acted as her father's secretary for such letters as came to him at his home address.

Humming to herself, Nancy curled up on the davenport and prepared to go through the mail.

"I'll ask Dad if he doesn't think my plan to find the Hutchinsons is a good one," she said to herself. "After all, he frequently has to hunt up missing witnesses and other folks and he may have a better scheme."

Nancy stripped the wrappers from the December magazines, which were already arriving, and placed the periodicals on the table. She discovered among the letters two envelopes addressed to herself, and with some dismay saw that one was unstamped and in the strong, angular handwriting of her father.

Nancy knew, even before she opened it, what the envelope contained. She had often found such messages from her parent, and always they contained the same announcement: "—an unexpected call out of town. I will not be home for two or three days."

Nancy's guess was partly correct.

As she drew out the folded note paper a new ten-dollar bill dropped from the envelope, a counterpart to the one she had just given Mrs. Sheets.

"Dear Nancy," she read, "I find I must go to the Capitol to review the case with the Governor and the State's Attorney, and to go through a number of records. I don't know how much time the job will require, but I feel sure you

will get along without me as you have at other
times. If I am not home by Saturday go ahead
with your plans for the game. Enclosed is a
little extra spending money for the occasion.
Affectionately, to say the least, C. D.''

Nancy tucked the money into her pocket.

She opened the other envelope addressed to
her. The handwriting was unfamiliar and the
postmark blurred, so it was with a little thrill
of anticipation that she unfolded the letter.
It read:

"My dear Miss Drew,

"Mr. Nickerson and I are very happy
that we shall have your company on the
trip to Emerson, and for the football game
and dramatics at the University. Ned has
told us a great deal about you and the exciting circumstances of your meeting.

"We plan to drive to the University next
Sunday, leaving soon after breakfast and
arriving at River Heights about 10 A.M.
If it is agreeable to you, will you be ready
at that time to join us the rest of the way?
I know it is unusually early for a Sunday
appointment, but we hope to complete the
trip before dark. I understand the young
women guests of the fraternity members
will be lodged at the Omega Chi Epsilon
house.

"If our plans do not accord with yours, there is plenty of time to alter them.

"Very sincerely,

"Edith (Mrs. James) Nickerson."

The rest of the mail, Nancy's practiced eye told her, consisted of advertisements and required no immediate attention.

Hannah, coming through the rooms to turn on the lights, greeted her young mistress.

"Mr. Drew came here about an hour ago and said he had to go to see the Governor," she announced, not without awe. "He put up his car and went by train, but he left a note for you, on the table."

"I found it, thank you, Hannah," Nancy said. "I am going upstairs to write a note. I have plenty of time before dinner, haven't I?"

"Yes, you have all of an hour," Hannah replied. "I'm sorry your father won't be here. I cooked the ducks you brought back from the farm, stuffed with apples the way he likes them. There'll be a lot wasted."

"Perhaps Bess or George will run over and help dispose of them," Nancy said. "I'll call them up."

She went to the telephone, but central said that there was no answer at the Marvin home. She next called George, who answered the telephone in person.

"Will I come to eat roast duckling?" she repeated. "Without a murmur. Too bad Bess is out of town."

"I'll expect you as soon as you can get here, then," Nancy said. "So long."

In her own little boudoir-sitting room Nancy sat down to compose an appropriate reply to Ned's mother. After some thought she wrote:

"Dear Mrs. Nickerson,

"It is very kind of you to include me in your party, and I accept with the greatest of pleasure the opportunity to drive to Emerson. I was most happy to get Ned's invitation for the big game, and I shall enjoy the Shakespearean play as much as the game, I know. I will be ready at 10 o'clock Sunday morning.

"Very sincerely,
"Nancy Drew."

"There," she thought. "Perhaps it is a little stiff, but it is better to be somewhat formal than too eager."

Nancy sealed the letter, stamped it and carried it downstairs.

"I'll mail it when I drive George home," she decided.

The next few moments Nancy spent looking over the evening paper, until a peal at the doorbell announced her dinner guest's arrival.

George, her cheeks rosy and her eyes sparkling from the keen November air, strode into the hallway and doffed her boyish ulster. Hat and muffler came off next, and George ran her fingers through her cropped hair until it crackled with electricity. She was proud of her masculine name, and dressed the part. Woe to the person who called her Georgette or even Georgie, let alone Georgiana or any other feminization of her real name!

"Bring on the ducks," she laughed, sniffing like a ravenous wolf. "Bones and all, and the feathers!"

"I'm sorry, but the feathers are off," Nancy said dolefully. "However, the ducks are stuffed with crab-apples, and that ought to make up for the other!"

Hannah announced dinner, and the girls went into the dining room, where George took Mr. Drew's seat at the table. Plates of clear tomato soup with brown crispy croutons were awaiting them, and without ado the girls began their meal.

"Dad always carves the ducks, chickens, turkeys and other birds," Nancy said somewhat dubiously. "Can you carve, George?"

"Carve? Why, I've been offered a position as chief surgeon at the General Hospital, I'm that handy with a knife," George boasted.

Nancy indicated to Hannah that the ducks were to be placed in front of George, and that self-assured young woman attacked them forthwith.

"Nancy, maybe you'd better hold this bird on the plate," she said after a few minutes of concentrated effort. "I don't think it was properly killed. A lot of life in it for a cooked du—hey! Get back, there!"

An especially energetic thrust with the carvng knife had caused the bird to skid to the edge of the platter. Nancy laughed until her sides ached.

"No, I'm just going to sit here and learn how the trick is done," she cried. "Maybe you could work better with a pair of shears?"

"I give up," George said ruefully.

Nancy appealed to Hannah.

"This is the way you do it," the housekeeper said, and with six slashes of the knife the bird was dismembered and great flaky slabs of breast-meat were heaped on the platter.

"It's all in knowing the combination, like opening a safe," George observed.

As the meal drew to a close George asked Nancy for an account of her day's sleuthing. In return, Nancy outlined to her the new mystery she was working on, that of locating the missing heiress.

"You follow the society news, don't you?"

Nancy asked her guest. "Do you recall ever having seen the name of Thomas Hutchinson? They must be a wealthy family if they employ governesses."

"Thomas Hutchinson—hm, let me see," George mused. "I don't remember any Thomas Hutchinson, but that last name is in the New York society columns a lot. It seems to me I read something about them recently."

"Oh, do try to remember when and where you read it," Nancy urged.

"That shouldn't be hard," George replied. "Let me think a moment. It must have been in a New York paper. Father subscribes to the Sunday edition of one of them, so that must be where I saw it. I haven't seen last Sunday's copy yet, so it must have been in the week before."

"I wonder where I can buy one," Nancy said.

"I think we still have it at home," George declared. "All the papers are piled in the basement for the collector, and I'm sure I can locate the article and clip it out for you."

"Will you do that for me?" cried Nancy. "It is bound to be a big help!"

The mystery of the missing Nancy was certainly clearing itself quickly, she thought. If only the more worrisome mystery of the missing mail pouch would solve itself as well!

CHAPTER XIII

CLUES AND CLOUDS

AFTER a pleasant evening of reminiscences and plans Nancy drove George to her home. On an impulse she returned by way of the railroad station to see if the news-stand there had, by any chance, a copy of the paper to which George had referred.

The stand, however, was closed and locked.

"I'll come here in the morning," Nancy resolved, and drove home.

She had a number of plans for the next day and embarked upon them early. For one thing, there was the matter of the new hat and slippers.

As she halted her car at the sidewalk in coming down the drive she was hailed by a woman whom she recognized as Mrs. Van Ness.

Nancy gave a guilty start. In the excitement of crowding events, she had forgotten all about sending Mrs. Van Ness the check for Ira Dixon's purse.

"Oh, Mrs. Van Ness, I feel ashamed of myself," she said, climbing out of her car. "But

you know that no sooner had you called me up
about the gift, than the bag was stolen from
Mr. Dixon here at the house.''

"That's perfectly all right," Mrs. Van Ness
smiled. "In fact, I called to you only to ask
if you had any news about poor Mr. Dixon.''

"I haven't, not the least bit," Nancy said
regretfully. "But now that we have met, may
I give my contribution toward the purse? He
will need the money now, I am sure.''

"Everybody has given two dollars," Mrs.
Van Ness said. "That, you see, will amount to
two hundred dollars altogether.''

Nancy tendered her crisp new ten-dollar bill,
and Mrs. Van Ness made the change.

"I hear that Mr. Dixon has more troubles
than one," she said, marking down Nancy's
contribution in a little note book. "Someone
seems to be after his inheritance.''

"I have heard rumors of that, too," Nancy
replied cautiously.

"A scoundrel of a step-brother, I hear,"
Mrs. Van Ness said. "Well, all of us who
know Mr. Dixon certainly wish him the best
of luck.''

Nancy agreed heartily to that wish as she
climbed back into her car. With the trail of
Nancy Smith Drew growing warmer Nancy
turned her thoughts more particularly upon
Ira Dixon's predicament.

"It's more than a hunch of mine that Edgar is the villain," she pondered as she headed for the shopping district. "In the first place, only Edgar has a grudge against Ira, at least as far as anybody knows. The man whom Tommy saw acting suspiciously returns to town the same day we know Edgar is visiting his stepbrother.

"I wish Ira was not so tender-hearted. He practically forbids me to work on my suspicion of Edgar. But who else could have done it?"

In the private parking area of the city's biggest department store Nancy left her car, and made her way to the millinery section.

"I'd like to see a sport hat," she told the young woman who stepped forward to wait on her. "Something in the Emerson colors, that I can wear with a raccoon coat."

Nancy seated herself before a mirror and soon the saleswoman returned with an assortment of hats.

"Some of these are in plain colors, but we could put a little plume on in the college colors," the clerk said.

Nancy at once rejected all the hats in solid orange, after surveying herself in one.

"I look like a pumpkin dressed up," she laughed. "They are too bright."

Finally she decided upon a snug-fitting felt of a deep rusty brown, which bore on one side a cluster of pheasant feathers. These she had replaced with a pair of quills in burnt orange color emerging from a fluff of violet down, thriftily retaining the pheasant feathers to put back on the hat after the university colors had served their purpose at the game.

Next she sought out the shoe department, and taking from her purse a scrap of the material of which her deep yellow evening gown was made, matched the color in silk dancing pumps.

Nancy proved herself to be a real girl, in that buying good-looking new clothes gave her a great thrill.

"I'd love to just wander around and look at all the pretty things," she said to herself, "but 1 must run down to the station and see if 1 can get a copy of that New York paper."

Tucking her purchases under her arm, Nancy reclaimed her car at the parking station and headed for the depot. The news-vendor informed her that he had a copy of last Sunday's newspaper in question, but none of the preceding week's.

"I get only six numbers, and New York tourists snap them up," he explained. "I got last Sunday's only yesterday and four of the six are gone already. Mostly it's New York folks homeward bound that get off here to stretch their legs while the engines are being changed who buy the New York papers. Seems as if they can't wait to read a home town paper, just as though we didn't have the same news in all the papers, north, south, east or west.''

As Nancy was not interested in the vagaries of the traveling public, she ended the lecture by buying one of the remaining copies of the paper in hopes that it, too, might make mention of the Hutchinson family.

''Whew, they certainly make these papers big enough,'' she marveled, as the clerk handed her a bulky bundle of newsprint and took her fifteen cents.

''Now for home,'' Nancy decided. ''It will take me the rest of the day to look through all these pages.''

More than one head was turned, in envy or admiration, to watch the pretty girl manipulate her snappy maroon car with the dash and confidence of a veteran driver. Traffic did not worry Nancy. She at all times followed implicitly the rule her father had taught her:

''Always signal when you are going to turn or stop, but drive yourself as if no other driver knew his signals. Remember it always takes two to make a collision.''

She smiled, as she saw a heavy sedan suddenly pull away from the curb, and noted that the man who was driving went straight ahead without glancing back or signalling. Courteously, Nancy allowed him to get into the stream of traffic ahead of her.

As she got a good view of the driver, she thought how much the fine-looking man looked like Ned Nickerson, only much older. and wondered if, by any chance, it could be Ned's father. The car with its red wheels, tan body and khaki-colored top fitted the description Ned had given her of his family's new car.

"It must be Mr. Nickerson driving. What a beautiful auto," thought Nancy as she idled behind the shining sedan. How quickly it responded to the touch of the accelerator, how easily it picked up speed when traffic moved on. It was certainly a fine piece of mechanism. Nancy kept close in her own sporty roadster, admiring every detail.

"This," she said to herself, "will no doubt be the car I'll ride in to Emerson, to see Ned play in that great football game on Founder's Day. It will be a decided change for me," she giggled aloud, "to sit on the back seat and be a guest for a change. In my newest clothes, too—like Cinderella."

The big car turned at the next corner, and as Nancy's route lay straight ahead the beautiful automobile was soon lost to view in the crowded thoroughfare.

She waved and smiled to one of her favorite traffic officers as she stepped firmly upon her own accelerator, eager to get home and unwrap her parcels and read that huge bundle of newspapers she had purchased.

Arriving at the Drew residence, Nancy first allowed herself the luxury of trying on her new hat with her fur coat to see the effect. Then she started the labor of going through the New York newspaper.

"I might as well discard everything except the general news and the society sections," she decided. "There won't be anything about the Hutchinsons in the comic pages, certainly, or the book reviews or magazine section."

Nancy settled herself upon the couch and began to scan the headlines. Her studies were interrupted by the telephone. It was George Fayne calling.

"I'm sorry, Nancy," she said, "but I don't think the Hutchinson item I saw will help you very much. I looked through the old papers and found it, and this is what it says:

" 'The annual Thanksgiving reunion of the Hutchinson Family will be held Thanksgiving Day as usual at the Hotel Van Kourtlandt. This is the twenty-ninth gathering, and it is expected that more than 125 persons will be present, all descendants of Jeffery Hutchinson, who settled in New York in 1652.'

"And that's all it says, Nancy."

"That's a help," Nancy declared. "Cer-

tainly among the 125 Hutchinsons there must
be the one who employed Nancy Drew.''

"Must be lots of Hutchinsons, though, who
are not from that branch of the family,'' George
said.

"The odds are with us just the same,'' Nancy
replied. "I'll write to the hotel and ask them
to put my request on the bulletin board. Thanks
a heap, George. You have helped me a lot.''

Nancy returned to her newspaper. She read
the social news section from the first column
to the last, but found no clue.

Then she turned to the general news sheets,
and on the third page a headline met her eyes
which made her sit bolt upright.

CHAPTER XIV

A FRESH PUZZLE!

*"Hutchinsons To Gather From Four Corners
Of the World For Traditional Thanksgiving"*

THE two column headlines marking what
newspaper editors call "a typical human-inter-
est story" topped a lengthy account, which
Nancy began reading from the first line.

"Even if I don't locate my particular Hutchinson," Nancy thought before she was half
way through, "this is certainly interesting."

The story related how one Jeffery Hutchinson had in the seventeenth century established
a farm above New York City boundaries, but
by the twentieth century its location was called
downtown. In the early days the population
of New York was predominantly Dutch, and
the patriotic Englishman had left a will in
which he stipulated that the old farm must never
be sold, but should forever be held jointly by
his heirs, and that once a year the family he
founded should meet "beneath the British
flag" to feast on the products of the farm.

The conditions of the will had been scrupulously obeyed, the newspaper story continued, but of course the flying of the British colors was now only a matter of form. Old Jeffery had not foreseen the day of an independent America.

"The products of the farm are no longer full ears of corn, golden pumpkins or rich cider," the item read. "Instead they consist of rents, golden coin and rich dividends. To-day the original acres constitute some of the most valuable real estate in the city, estimated to produce a revenue of many millions of dollars a year which the lineal descendants of Old Jeffery share."

The romance of the story almost made Nancy forget the reasons for her interest in the Hutchinson family, until a name caught her attention.

"The family treasurer who will present the heads of all the Hutchinson clans with their checks on Thanksgiving Day is Thomas Jeffery Hutchinson of Palm Beach, Cape Cod and Fifth Avenue."

"That's the man I'm looking for," Nancy decided, her heart glowing with success.

She started upstairs to write Mr. Hutchinson a letter, when Hannah announced luncheon. If the truth must be told, Nancy bolted her food at that meal, scarcely tasting what she ate.

At last she pushed away her dessert half-eaten and flew up the stairs to compose her message of request to Thomas Hutchinson, but no sooner had she taken up her pen, than there was a ringing of the doorbell.

Nancy cocked an ear and heard Hannah expostulating with some stranger. Then the housekeeper slowly climbed the stairs and thrust her head into the doorway of Nancy's room.

"It's that crazy woman again," the housekeeper said with a sigh. "I told her to go away, but she says she won't budge until she has seen you."

"Tell her I'm too busy to see her," Nancy ordered.

"I did," Hannah said in a grieved tone. "But she said you're just puttin' her off——"

"Anything else?"

"I sort of hate to say it, it's that impudent, but the old witch said she knew you were too lazy to walk down the stairs, that's what she said," Hannah concluded.

A flush of vexation colored Nancy's cheeks, and her eyes flashed dangerously.

"I'll talk to her," she said, jumping up from her chair and hurrying down to the hall ahead of Hannah.

Mrs. Sheets was standing with her back to the closed door.

"I knew you'd see me," she crowed as Nancy appeared.

"What do you want?" Nancy demanded.

"As I told you once afore, I don't want nothing except what's mine by right," Mrs. Sheets said.

"You can expect nothing more from me, then," Nancy replied.

"Don't get hitey-titey, my lady," Mrs. Sheets cried, shaking a finger at Nancy. "You may regret it. I came here on an errand of good-will, but if you don't show proper respect for your elders I'll go away and you'll learn nothing."

"Mrs. Sheets, I do respect persons who command my respect," Nancy retorted. "But it seems all I hear from you is scolding, and I have done nothing to gain your ill-will."

"Tut tut, young people don't get scolded half enough," the woman asserted boldly. "When I was your age I wasn't too old to be taken across my mother's knees for a sound spanking if I didn't keep a civil tongue in my head for my elders. That's what's wrong with the world today, I do declare. The chicks with pinfeathers thinks they can teach the old birds to fly. As I always say to Mrs. Maroni next door, who has eight young ones, 'Mrs. Maroni,' I says——"

"You may not believe it, but I have important work to do," Nancy interrupted. "Won't you please tell me why you came to see me?"

"Work! I like that!" Mrs. Sheets laughed. "You look as if you was scrubbin' floors or sweepin', I must say. Well, I came to tell you all them missin' letters was mailed back to their owners!"

Nancy took a step back, her hand to her throat. Surprise, delight, incredulity, made her speechless for the moment.

"Aha, I thought that would knock you over," Mrs. Sheets cried. "Now maybe you'll tell that upstart maid of yours I had a right to see you."

"Tell me how you know they were all mailed to their destinations again," Nancy asked.

"Well, this morning the new letter man—a fine smart young man, too, not an old busy-body like Dixon—came to the door and handed me three letters," Mrs. Sheets went on, enjoying her triumph. "And the first one was the gas bill, which was away too high. We're folks for early sleepin', and I never burned no four dollars worth of gas last month and the company is going to hear from me, I tell you.

"The next letter wasn't a letter at all, by rights, but a postcard from an old neighbor of mine in New York, only she lives in Florida now. She bought a lot of land during the boom down there and now it ain't worth half what she paid, but she hasn't any money no more and so she lives on it, and she says what the rich people find in Florida she can't——"

"Oh, Mrs. Sheets, please!" Nancy cried. "What has all this to do with the case?"

"I'm coming to it, ain't I?" Mrs. Sheets demanded. "Just give me time.

"As I was saying—where was I now? See, you made me forget! Well, never mind. The other letter, mind you, was from Joe's sister and I knew right well she wouldn't write twice a week if somebody held her hand to guide the pen. And there was ten dollars in the letter, too, and she wouldn't send me twenty dollars in one week any more than she would send me a million. So I got an idea and I looked at the postmark, and sure enough, it was stamped twice at our post office here!

"There was one mark dated three days ago, and one dated yesterday afternoon!"

"Oh, won't Mr. Dixon be happy!" Nancy cried. "I'm so glad. It is the best news I have heard in a long time. Thank you ever so much, Mrs. Sheets."

"Oh, you sing a different tune now, don't you?" jeered the disagreeable woman. "I thought you'd come down off your high horse. Well, anyhow, here is your ten dollars."

She suddenly thrust out a dirty hand, which clasped a wadded bill.

"I'd rather you kept it, Mrs. Sheets," Nancy said. "You may have it."

"Huh, do I look like I took charity?" snapped the woman, tossing the money on the floor. "There it is, and if you want to leave it for the sweeper it's none of my concern."

"I didn't mean to offend you," Nancy cried. "I am sorry if you misunderstood me."

"It just goes to prove what I said, that modern young folks has no manners," Mrs. Sheets snapped. "Well, anyhow, the lady next door came running over and told me she had got a letter that should have come in the mail that you say Dixon got robbed of, so I guess all of them was mailed."

"It certainly seems so," Nancy cried. "I shall tell the postmaster at once, so he can make inquiries at the other houses on the route."

"I guess you had your fun," Mrs. Sheets said with a smirk, as she turned the knob of the door.

"What do you mean?" Nancy demanded.

"Oh, I can see how two or three young girls of this day and age might think it too funny for words to steal a poor old man's mail bag and hide the letters from the rightful owners for a day or two," the woman snapped. "I'm not so blind I can't see through a knot-hole."

Nancy's new-found toleration of the woman vanished in the wrath her insinuation provoked.

"You certainly have a totally wrong impression," she cried. "Neither I nor my friends would be guilty of such a low trick!"

"Maybe so, maybe so," Mrs. Sheets said as she stepped from the house. "I can't help having my thoughts, though. But I won't say anything. Don't think I'll spread any gossip. Goodbye!"

She slammed the door and was gone.

Nancy leaned against the wall as her anger gave way to sudden mirth.

"What a woman," she said aloud. "I certainly don't blame Sailor Joe for taking long voyages."

She picked up the bank-note from the floor and went directly to the telephone. First she called up Ira Dixon and told him the good news. Then she informed Postmaster Cutter.

"I'll send tracers out at once to see if letters were remailed to other homes," he assured Nancy. "But this makes the matter more puzzling than before! Why should anyone steal the mail and then go to the risk and pains of remailing it?"

"I think, Mr. Cutter," Nancy said, "that you will find personal malice at the bottom of it. The mail was not stolen for any valuables it contained but to wreck the reputation of Mr. Dixon."

"It seems to me you know a lot about the

whole affair," Cutter barked through the telephone.

"I know no more than anybody else," Nancy answered. "I am just using common sense."

"I suppose that means the detectives and Secret Service men are not using common sense?" the official sneered. "Well, Miss, I think I'll have one of them question you—just to get your advice on how to catch the thief, of course!"

"Any time at all," Nancy replied, and cut the conversation short by hanging up the receiver.

"And now, perhaps, I can finish my letter," she sighed thoughtfully.

Hannah had been standing in the kitchen doorway, and though she was not naturally of an inquisitive nature, yet she could not resist inquiring of Nancy if Sailor Joe's wife had really brought the ten-dollar bill back so soon.

"Yes, she did," said Nancy with a laugh. "Would you believe it, she did not hand it to me, but threw it on the floor?"

"Well, I hope she never comes again. I don't want to open the front door and find her hateful, dirty face looking at me. I wouldn't let her in!"

"Never mind." said Nancy, "the incident is closed. She will have no reason to come here again."

Hannah took up her dust-cloth, set to work with unusual vigor, and Nancy knew that the thoughts of the sailor's wife were the stimuli for Hannah's energy.

"I am going upstairs to write an important letter," announced Nancy as she started toward her own room, where she hoped to be able to concentrate on a suitable letter to Thomas Hutchinson of New York.

"The sooner that gets mailed, the nearer I'll be to the solution of my other mystery," she said to herself.

Entering her own room, Nancy recalled the remarks of Sailor Joe's wife about Nancy and her friends having stolen the mail-bag. Was it possible she had put such an idea into the Postmaster's head? Mr. Cutter's remark about sending the officials to see Nancy would make it seem so.

A new worry was shaping itself in the mind of Nancy Drew.

CHAPTER XV

OFF TO EMERSON

THE rest of the week dragged slowly for Nancy. There was not time for a reply to be received from Mr. Hutchinson, and one problem in the mail case had solved itself by the return of the stolen letters.

"Now I'd like to discover Ira's mail pouch for him," Nancy planned.

As yet there was not the slightest clue to work upon.

George and Bess came to the Drew home and duly admired Nancy's additions to her wardrobe. Nancy tried on her evening frock with the new slippers for her chums, and they agreed that the color ensemble would be perfect with a corsage of real hot-house violets.

"Ned will be real proud of you," George laughed. "I wager he'll be so busy watching you in the stands that he won't keep his eye on the ball."

"If I were to wear this evening gown to the football game, I'd believe that," Nancy laughed. "Ned would not be the only one,

either. And I, instead of seeing the play that
night, would be seeing the inside of a hospital
probably!''

"I'd almost be green with envy over you,"
Bess commented, "only the one thing that
saves my finer feelings is that we're going to
Grandma's for dinner, George and I, for a
family reunion. And Grandma raises turkeys
—umm-m-m!''

"Speaking of family reunions," Nancy said,
"I found out about the Hutchinsons."

She located the clipping she had cut from
the newspaper and gave it to George to read
aloud.

"I've written to that Thomas Jeffery Hutchinson mentioned there," Nancy added. "I'm
sure we'll learn something about the missing
Nancy and restore her to her estate."

At last the end of the week arrived. Saturday dawned gray and rainy, and Nancy's
spirits fell at the prospect of a wet and dreary
week-end.

Sunday morning, though, she was awakened
by a brilliant sun streaming in through her
windows, accompanied by a brisk and biting
breeze. It was an ideal late Autumn day, the
brilliance of the sky holding promise of continued fair weather.

Nancy spent no time day dreaming but was
out of bed and preparing for her trip. She had

packed her suitcase on the preceding night, and had laid out the clothing she planned to wear on the journey.

By nine o'clock breakfast was finished, and there remained a whole hour to be spent before Mr. and Mrs. Nickerson would arrive from Mapleton.

Joyous whistles from the river told of the first of the excursion steamers leaving for Emerson. Nancy had seen them sail away other years and could picture the three-decked stern-wheelers, masts and ratlines flaunting the colors of the rival universities.

Ten o'clock struck, and impatiently Nancy donned her new hat and stood at the front door, her raccoon coat over her arms.

Just then a sleek, long-nosed tan sedan with khaki-colored top and red wheels appeared, driving close to the curb at a snail's pace. The driver seemed to be scanning the house numbers. Nancy was not disappointed. The automobile stopped at her door.

For a moment she was undecided whether primly to await Mr. Nickerson in the hall or to run out and greet the couple at the curb. Instinct prevailed, and hastily donning her coat Nancy opened the door and sped down the flagged path to the automobile, just as the front door of the car opened. A man stepped out.

"Are you Miss Drew?" he smiled.

"I am Nancy Drew—and you must be Mr. Nickerson," Nancy cried.

"That is who I am," the man bowed, removing his hat and smiling as he opened the rear door of the sedan.

"This is Miss Drew, Mother," he said. "Mrs. Nickerson, Miss Drew."

Nancy had anticipated this meeting with a little misgiving, but she was immediately put at her ease by Mrs. Nickerson, and Ned's father reminded her much of her own parent.

"Won't you come into the house for a moment's rest?" Nancy invited. "I am sorry that Dad is not here. I am alone."

"Thank you, no," Mrs. Nickerson smiled. "If we may we will stop on our return trip, but I think the sooner we start for Emerson the more we are likely to escape traffic."

"Then I shall get my bag and be with you at once," Nancy said, and ran to the house. Hannah, in a crisp new uniform, was waiting at the door for her, and stepped out on the porch to give Nancy her suitcase.

"Have a good time," the faithful housekeeper cried.

"I will!" Nancy answered.

Mr. Nickerson came up the path to take Nancy's bag, and stowed it in the front of the car, where two other expensive-looking grips were piled. Nancy seated herself beside Mrs.

Nickerson, who spread a robe over the girl's lap.

While Mr. Nickerson turned the car about, Nancy took stock of her escorts. Ned's father was a man between forty-five and fifty, with iron grey hair and keen blue eyes, a wide, humorous mouth and a firm chin. Ned resembled him very much, Nancy decided.

Mrs. Nickerson was a tiny woman. Nancy believed she could stand upright beneath her son's outstretched arm. She was extraordinarily young-looking, blue-eyed also, with a clear, unwrinkled skin and beautiful snow-white hair, prematurely so from its heaviness and vitality. Nancy decided she would look very attractive in evening dress.

"What a lovely street, lined with those grand old sycamores," Mrs. Nickerson was saying. "You have a lovely home, Nancy. May I call you Nancy?"

"Please do," the girl cried. "I haven't been called 'Miss Drew' very long, and I can't get used to it."

"Nancy, I expect you to help me drive," Mr. Nickerson called from the front. "I am not one to object to back-seat driving. Mrs. Nickerson will tell you I have a perfect genius for taking the wrong turn no matter how often I have traveled the road, and this one I haven't driven over for two years."

Nancy kept her eyes on all the direction signs and concluded that Mr. Nickerson had exaggerated his incompetence, for he drove swiftly and surely on the right road for Emerson.

At one o'clock the half-way mark was celebrated with luncheon at a charming old tavern, and now there were so many cars on the road flaunting the pennants of the rival colleges that there was no need of straying from the right route.

Just before sunset the towers of Emerson University came into view above the trees on its ancient campus. Traffic was so dense that progress was made but slowly. Ned had reserved parking space for his father at a local garage and had mailed the ticket. To the surprise and delight of the party Ned himself was posted at the garage door. With a war-whoop of welcome he charged the car and helped his mother and Nancy to alight.

"Welcome to Emerson!" he shouted in high spirits.

Nancy felt a thrill of pride as she heard some bystanders comment, "That's Nickerson, the sensational sophomore quarter-back! He'll be on the All-American before he closes his career."

"It isn't far to where you are going to stay," Ned said, a grip under each arm and a suitcase in one hand. "I have to eat at the training table so I can't have dinner with you all. Gosh, isn't it grand weather?"

"I'm sure I'm going to have a thrilling time on my visit," Nancy cried.

"Oh, I hope you will," Ned answered.

Nancy did not realize just then how thrilling a time lay before her.

CHAPTER XVI

A Surprise in the Stadium

The Omega Chi Epsilon House was one of a dozen fraternity buildings facing the west side of the Emerson campus.

Every one of the frat houses resembled a bee hive. Women and girls were clustered on the verandas, looking through the windows and entering or leaving the buildings in a constant procession.

Nancy felt happy and gay. The excitement of the crowds, the air of anticipation that hung over the college town, wiped from her mind for the time being all vexatious mysteries.

"Here we are," Ned said, leading his little party up a walk to a brick building in Colonial style, from the upper floor windows of which floated three huge banners, the Stars and Stripes, the orange and purple university banner and a white flag with the Greek letters of the fraternity in green.

Nancy and Ned's parents followed the young man through the chattering throng to the broad staircase, where a colored man in a white jacket relieved Ned of the luggage.

"Here's your room, Nancy," Ned said, as they reached the second floor. The door was open and Nancy recognized Helen Corning among the people in the room.

Greetings and introductions were exchanged. Helen's mother and Buck Rodman's parents were there as well as Buck himself, a sturdy, curly-haired chap whom Ned identified as assistant manager of the football team and a member of the baseball and basketball teams.

Hotel reservations had been made for the parents, and soon the older folks left to be escorted to their quarters by the boys. They were all to meet in an hour for dinner.

"Isn't this the most thrilling time you have had in all your life?" Helen demanded, when the girls were alone. "Shall we toss to see who uses the mirror first? Which bed would you rather have?"

"My answer to all three questions is 'yes,' " Nancy laughed.

Dinner was served in the university dining hall. Buck joined the party there, but Ned, of course, had to eat at the gymnasium with the rest of the football squad, whose diet was strictly supervised.

Conversation was limited to football exclusively. Buck explained that the game was not only in settlement of ancient rivalries renewed each year, but would determine the championship of the Middle West.

"Out on the coast Standford is still unbeaten, and in the east Yarmouth has won every game but the one it plays next Saturday with Horning," he explained. "If we win tomorrow we shall be able to claim being one of the best teams in the country."

Ned joined the group after dinner and escorted Nancy and his parents on a tour of inspection. He showed them the recitation halls, the observatory, the university museum, and the evening concluded with everyone attending services at the chapel.

Bedtime came all too quickly, but it seemed to Nancy that she had barely touched her head to the pillow before tolling bells awakened her to crisp sunlight and the day of the big game.

With Helen, Nancy waited on the steps of the fraternity house for Buck, who was going to escort the girls to the hotel for breakfast.

"It's just a perfect day," the girls agreed.

"I hope the wind dies down a little," Buck frowned with a professional air. "It's blowing at right angles to the field and will spoil the kicking."

Nancy did not see Ned until after luncheon, just before the party started for the stadium. He escorted them to the proper entrance and excused himself, for he had to get into uniform and listen to the final exhortations of the coach.

"My goodness, what a crowd," Mrs. Nickerson exclaimed.

"The stadium holds 25,000," Mr. Nickerson said, "and I understand all the seats were sold out three days ago. A special train was run from Chicago to accommodate the crowds from that neighborhood, and the East. Even airplanes were bringing spectators from the West and the South."

Mr. Nickerson spread rugs on the concrete seats for Nancy and his wife, and Helen and her mother were similarly provided for by Mr. Rodman. Across the field the State University cheering section was thundering forth its defiance, and the band played with more energy than music. Pennants were waving everywhere.

Suddenly Buck appeared in the aisle.

"I had a minute to spare, so I thought I'd see that you were all fixed," he said, squeezing himself between Nancy and Helen.

He had brought programs with him for everybody and pointed out Ned's name and number on the score card.

"You won't recognize him in his pads and helmet from up here," Buck explained, "but you can tell him by his number—32.   Our fellows wear purple jerseys with orange numerals.''

He chatted on about the team and its methods, and then pointed suddenly to a group in the row in front, and a little to the right, of Nancy's party.

''That's Clifford Doolittle, the captain of the team,'' he whispered, pointing to a very tall, red-haired young man beneath whose overcoat could be seen the trappings of a football player.

''That must be his fiancée he is talking with,'' Buck went on, sotto voce. ''I guess Coach Hart gave him permission to come out, seeing it's the last game he'll ever play here. She's a very wealthy girl from the East. I forget her name.''

Nancy looked with interest at the captain and his pretty escortee, a girl a few years older than herself, exquisitely dressed. The football player seemed reluctant to leave her, but finally turned to go.

The young woman evidently thought of something important to tell Doolittle, for she ran after him, calling his name. As she did so her purse dropped, falling almost at Nancy's feet.

When Doolittle finally left Nancy leaned over and tapped the girl on the shoulder.

''Your purse—you dropped it,'' she said.

"Oh, how careless of me—and how good of
you," smiled the young woman. "Thank you."

Then the thunder of cheers and applause
which rocked the stadium as the teams trotted
on the field made further conversation impossible.

A whistle was blown by the white-garbed
referee, and the captains of the opposing teams
met to confer with the officials. The two elevens lined up.

"Emerson receives the kick!" Mr. Nickerson
said, "but I don't see Ned."

Then the ball sailed through the air, descended to the arms of an alert Emerson half-
back, and the game was on.

Never did two teams seem more evenly
matched. The linesmen held like concrete walls,
and neither team could gain on rushes. The
few forward passes that were attempted were
knocked down by alert ends or backs, and the
first quarter ended with the score 0 to 0.

During the brief intermission between quarters a young man, evidently past his college
years, worked his way across to the young
woman whose purse Nancy had restored.

"Hello, Marion," he called to her. "What
are you doing so far from your family's high
jinks?"

Nancy heard the girl call back to him:

"Don't you think Cliff's biggest game of his career is more important than that?"

The man finally edged his way to the young woman's side and Nancy, without purposely eavesdropping, heard "New York" and "Thanksgiving" mentioned, before the resumption of the game claimed her full attention.

"If she is wealthy and from New York she may know the Hutchinsons," flashed through Nancy's mind. "I must ask her before we leave."

The two teams continued their struggle.

Some minutes passed and then Nancy saw a familiar figure dash from the side-lines and report to the referee. When he turned she saw a big orange 32 on his back, and knew that Ned had at last got into the game.

"Just to give the regular quarter-back a rest," Ned's father guessed, and correctly. Farquhar, the veteran quarter-back, was one of the best known players in the country, and Ned's chances of appearing in the initial line-up were slim until Farquhar should graduate.

The game took on a new interest to the party, now that Ned was in it. Nancy hoped that somehow Ned would streak down the field for a touchdown, but the half ended with both teams still scrapping doggedly in mid-field.

It was a long intermission, during which both

elevens retired to their dressing rooms, giving the stadium over to the cheering sections and bands of the respective colleges.

Nancy watched with fascination as the uniformed bands marched and countermarched, playing each other's school songs and anthems out of courtesy and maneuvering to spell out the colleges' initials. Then she remembered the young woman from the East, and leaned over to attract her attention.

"Please excuse me," Nancy said, "but I was told you are from New York. This may sound silly, because I know how many millions of people live in New York, but do you by any chance know a family named Hutchinson?"

The young woman looked surprised.

"I—why, that is *my* name!"

Nancy could scarcely refrain from exclaiming her surprise, but checked herself.

"I have a very special reason for asking," Nancy said. "It concerns the welfare of a person who is missing. Are you related to Thomas J. Hutchinson?"

The girl looked at Nancy quizzically.

"He is my father," she said.

CHAPTER XVII

THE YELLOW COAT

No sooner had the girl spoken than the people on all sides rose to their feet with a roar. The two teams were surging forth upon the field again.

Miss Hutchinson's lips moved, but Nancy could not hear a word she said. Finally the young woman shook her head and signaled to Nancy that she would speak with her after the game.

The teams lined up for the kick-off.

"Ned's on the sidelines again," Mr. Nickerson said, disappointment in his voice.

"His chance will come again," Nancy declared with confidence.

Emerson kicked, and the men were down the field like whippets, downing the State player who caught the ball, before he had taken two steps.

The excitement was tremendous in all sections of the stands, but the Emerson rooters soon grew glum. A shifting wind played havoc with the ball, and an early lead by Ned's team was easily lost. Then came luck for Emerson's opponents, and presently a State man carried the ball over the goal line, the kick was made, and the score stood:

State University 7—Emerson 0.

During the rest of the quarter neither team scored, and at the end Nancy hoped to get a chance to talk further to the attractive Marion Hutchinson. That young lady was surrounded by a crowd of friends, however, and Nancy feared that in the excitement the young New Yorker would not realize the importance of finding the heir to the property in England. As a matter of fact, the eyes of Miss Hutchinson had been fixed continuously during the game on Clifford Doolittle, the red-haired captain.

"Such luck," groaned Mr. Nickerson, pulling up his coat collar and slouching down in his seat, as the whistle blew for the beginning of the last quarter.

By sheer desperation the home team finally succeeded in forcing the State team back to its 30-yard line and there was held.

As the umpire's horn tooted, Nancy rose to her feet with an impulsive cheer, for Ned had darted out upon the field and was reporting.

Emerson's players went into a huddle.

Presently from the State cheering sections came the rhythmic chant:

"Block that kick! Block that kick!"

Nancy sat, tense and unwinking, her fingers gripped tight, as Ned stood on the thirty-five yard line, his arms outstretched.

The ball was snapped.

Down charged the State players, bowling over the Emerson men and converging upon Ned. As coolly as if he were alone on the field Ned measured the distance to the goal, dropped the ball and with a powerful thrust of his toe sent it spinning between the posts, just as the charging enemy piled on top of him.

State University 7—Emerson 3!

Four minutes left to play! The entire stadium was now a boiling mass of humanity, with both sides shouting, cheering, yelling, calling for another score. But nothing happened for the next three minutes to change the score.

"Ned's still in there!" Nancy shouted. "He wasn't called back!"

Ten yards to go, with now only one minute to play!

Emerson lined up. Ned clapped his hands. Doolittle, the full-back, stood far behind the line as if to receive the ball for a kick.

The ball was snapped, and then there was nothing to be seen but a confusion of flying arms and legs.

"Look, look! A fake kick! They're going around end!"

Everyone was screaming, shouting.

A third of the State team was lying on top of Doolittle, who was expected to kick but had not received the ball. The rest of the State men not sprawling on the ground were pursuing a knot of Emerson men sweeping around left end.

Ned, with one other team-mate, was standing upright, surveying the melee around him as if he were only an interested spectator.

"The boy must have gone insane!" Mr. Nickerson fumed. "I wonder if he was kicked in the head?"

The runners went down under the charge of the State University men, and then all of a sudden Ned and his companion broke into a run.

As if pursued by lions they streaked for the enemy goal line.

"A double fake! They have the ball!" howled the spectators, in delight or dismay according to their sides.

One of the State men wheeled and charged after Ned and his team-mate, heading them off. A phenomenally fast runner, he was soon at their heels and launched himself at Ned, who was carrying the ball which he had held concealed between his knees while the fake plays were being run.

Ned tossed the ball to his companion as the opponent's arms encircled his hips. Unimpeded, the player dashed over the State goal for the winning score. Ned kicked the goal, and Emerson was victorious by a score of 10 to 7.

Nancy found herself being hugged by Mr. Nickerson and an utterly strange, middle-aged woman. In front of her a man was jumping on his own hat with every sign of delight in his strange performance.

In the turmoil Nancy lost sight of Miss Hutchinson. When the tumult died down a little later and the throng poured on the field for the triumphant snake dance, she caught sight of the young woman moving toward the exit, and deserting her party Nancy ran after her.

It was no easy task for Nancy to elbow her way through the milling throng. Every one around her was in a happy frame of mind since the home town team had won. Little did this lively crowd dream that this slip of a girl was working diligently even at this time to find a certain young woman lost to her friends and relatives in England.

It was a big task Nancy had set herself, but she intended following every clue to its source —she would not fail. She would overtake the beautiful Miss Hutchinson and question her at once. She hoped she could reach her in time.

Broad backs, heavy fur coats, robes, streamers, hats and vendors seemed to make Nancy's progress a snail's pace. She craned her neck to keep in sight the young woman who was nearing the exit. Steadfastly she battled with the wild congestion before her, but kept edging closer and closer to the open gates. At last she drew a deep breath, lifted her head high and called, "Miss Hutchinson—Miss Hutchinson."

No answer came back, as apparently the call had not been heard. Again Nancy plunged through the crowd toward the young woman, wondering what Mr. and Mrs. Nickerson must be thinking of her strange disappearance. She was determined, however, not to lose this valuable opportunity to solve the contents of her mysterious letter from England. She could explain and apologize later to her friends.

"Miss Hutchinson!" she cried. "Please wait!"

The girl heard her and halted, smiling.

"I must explain to you," Nancy panted. "I am looking for a young woman who once worked in your family as a governess."

"Do you mean Nancy Drew?"

"Yes," Nancy replied. "You see, oddly enough, my name is the same as hers, except for the Smith in the middle. She has come into a fortune in England and in trying to locate her the estate found me, because our names are alike."

"I'm so glad for Miss Drew," Miss Hutchinson exclaimed. "But I don't know how I can help. She studied for the stage, you know, and was with us only for two years before she joined a company giving Shakespearean revivals on tour, and I never heard from her again."

Nancy's hopes were dashed. She felt as bleakly disappointed as if State University had downed Ned in his tracks on his victorious dash to the goal-line.

"I'm sorry," Miss Hutchinson added. "Dreadfully sorry. Perhaps Father knows where she is. I shall ask him when I go home. We all loved Miss Drew and would do anything to restore her to her inheritance."

"Will you see your father as soon as you arrive in New York?" asked Nancy eagerly.

"I think so, unless Father has been called away to a conference at Washington."

"I hope not," responded Nancy. "I do so want to find the girl and bring her this happiness before it is too late."

"I agree with you. I want to help, too," asserted the lovely girl. "I'll do all I can to assist you in locating her so that you can give Miss Drew this important information."

"Thank you ever so much," Nancy said, a little more cheerful now. "Will you be at the play tonight?"

"Indeed yes, and I hope I'll see you there,"

Marion Hutchinson said. "I will look for you, and we may be able to make some plans together."

Nancy turned to struggle back to Mrs. Nickerson, who was watching with keen amusement the antics of the Emerson supporters on the field. Her husband had joined them.

Two men in heated argument blocked the aisle through which Nancy had to pass.

"You pay me that bet, or you'll be sorry!" one of the men, a short, red-faced fellow, bellowed.

"Go on, I bet that—excuse me, Miss," said the other chap. "Here, let the lady pass."

As Nancy brushed by the arguing men something strikingly familiar about the second speaker made her pause and look at him again.

His face was half concealed by a brilliant muffler, above which only a sharp nose protruded. Pulled down over his eyes was a gray cap, and he wore a yellow overcoat!

CHAPTER XVIII

The Scent Grows Hotter

"Light cap and yellow overcoat——"

That was the description given by small Tommy of the man who had been sneaking around the house the day the mail was stolen.

And the sharp, long nose—it recalled to Nancy the face on the snapshot of Ira Dixon's brother.

She heard Mrs. Nickerson, laughter in her voice, calling to her. Nancy hesitated for a moment and then boldly stepped up to the arguing pair.

"Excuse me, please," she began, touching the sleeve of the yellow overcoat. "May I speak to you a moment? My name is Miss Drew——"

The man shrank back.

"Sorry, I can't be bothered," he said, drawing his coat collar closer about his face. "Come on, Harris, we'll settle this some place else."

He turned and leaped down the concrete steps to the field below, followed by his companion, who paused to stare at Nancy with wonderment and then bolted after his vanishing enemy.

"Now what shall I do?" thought the vexed girl, as she turned to rejoin Mrs. Nickerson.

That person was anxiously waiting to point out to Nancy how Ned, his jersey in tatters, was being carried around the field on the shoulders of a cheering throng of alumni and undergraduates.

"Poor Ned, he detests that sort of thing," his mother laughed. "But didn't he play splendidly?"

"He practically won the game single-handed," Nancy replied warmly. "He'll be a hero, with his name and picture in every newspaper in the country, I know."

"You and I are just out of it, that's all," Mrs. Nickerson smiled. "What shall we do? Would you like to come to the hotel with me, and we'll have some hot tea and cakes in the lounge until the men rejoin us?"

Mrs. Rodman and Mrs. Corning, together with Helen, were also standing, deserted by Buck and Mr. Rodman who were on the field dancing and celebrating.

Mrs. Nickerson repeated her invitation to the three other women, and it was enthusiastically accepted. The five, joining forces, found an exit and joined the crowd moving through the

streets of Emerson toward boat landing, automobile parks and flying field.

As the group walked along they exchanged
comments on the beauty of the college town.

"Emerson has no railroad, you know," Mrs.
Rodman said. "I think that has kept it from
getting spoiled. It is just a college town, with
no other pretensions."

At the hotel festive groups were re-living the
thrilling moments that closed the big game.
Ned's name was on every lip. A group of men
identified as radio announcers, who had broad-
cast the play-by-play account of the game over
the country, were hoarsely congratulating one
another on having been assigned to that particular contest instead of being kept in reserve
for a Thanksgiving Day or Saturday contest in
some other corner of the nation.

It was a hopeless quest to find a waitress free
to serve tea, and the party adjourned to the
sitting room of Mrs. Nickerson's suite. There
they chatted of football, of clothes and other
friendly topics until they were all five drawn
to the window by a sustained roaring and
cheering.

Ned, a patch of court-plaster over one eye,
was struggling in the hands of an enthusiastic,
hero-worshipping throng. The watchers saw
him point to the hotel and plead with the men
who insisted upon making him the head of a

parade. At last he lowered his head and charged through the throng, and a few minutes later he burst panting into the room, where his mother hugged him and the others added their praise.

"Great guns," the embarrassed youth protested. "It took twenty men to win that game, counting all the substitutes. The quarter-back always gets a lot of praise he doesn't deserve, just because he has to handle the ball. What are the chances of something to eat?"

Mrs. Nickerson called the hotel restaurant on the 'phone and when she repeated that it was the hero of the afternoon's game and his friends who wanted refreshments a waitress was at the door in five minutes with a well-stocked tea-wagon. Mr. Nickerson, somewhat disheveled and minus his hat, entered in time for tea and cakes.

The entire group remained together for dinner at the hotel, and then Buck and Ned escorted the girls back to the fraternity house that they might dress for the dance and theater party.

Helen proposed a half hour's nap, and Nancy was glad of the opportunity to do a little thinking. In the darkened room she dismissed—not without difficulty—football from her mind and concentrated on the unexpected developments in her two mystery cases.

"There is no use worrying about Nancy Smith Drew," she said to herself. "She is probably somewhere in the East, and now that I know she is engaged in theatrical work, why all that remains is to advertise in one or all of the professional papers and magazines.

"On the other hand, was the man in the yellow coat Edgar Dixon? If not, why did he run away?"

Nancy cudgeled her brains for some way of apprehending the man under suspicion.

"I guess it is hopeless trying to find him in this crowd," she thought. "And what charges can I bring against him? The police would want some evidence on which to arrest him, and if it were the wrong man I would get into trouble."

Nancy knew, from association with her lawyer father, that it is a serious thing to have a person falsely arrested.

She dressed for the evening without having reached a decision in the matter.

Emerson's big gymnasium was converted into a theater for the evening. After the performance the chairs were to be removed and the dance would be held on the same floor.

"As closely as possible," Nancy read from her program as she sat in the improvised auditorium, "the stage of Shakespeare's time will be imitated. As in the days of the Bard of

Avon the audience will surround the players, and there will be no scenery."

The English Department of the University was staging the revival, with the cast from the membership of the Emerson Wig and Buskin Society, the Dramatic Club of the University.

Nancy was interrupted by a tap on her shoulder. She turned to see Marion Hutchinson seated behind her, looking beautiful in an orchid evening dress, and wearing a necklace of amethysts and diamonds.

"May I present Clifford Doolittle?" Marion asked. "All this sitting next to me is he, both of him."

She laughed, and fondly regarded the huge form at her right. Doolittle looked even larger in evening dress than in his football togs.

Nancy smiled her acknowledgment of the introduction, and then her attention was claimed by Ned, who sat down beside her.

"Hello, Cliff," he greeted his captain. "I just begged off from my part in the play. I had a job as one of the crowd in the courtroom, but I think I'll do better as one of the crowd in the audience."

Cliff introduced Ned to Marion Hutchinson, and then the lights were lowered and the play began.

Nancy was fascinated. She had never seen a play given in the old Shakespearean manner.

It was almost like being a part of the drama itself, with the actors lolling about among the audience awaiting their cues.

At the end of the first act all the players mingled with their friends in the audience. It was most unusual and amusing.

Nancy turned to her program to try to identify the various characters. She was amazed how well some of the feminine roles were impersonated by the college boys.

Her eyes, scanning the dramatis personae, suddenly caught sight of a name that looked so familiar it made her hand tremble. The lights suddenly went out and Nancy had to await the end of the second act before she could make sure her eyes had not deceived her.

Meanwhile she laughed at Launcelot Gobbo and fidgeted while the Duke of Aragon was deciding which of the three caskets to choose, but through it all she held the program open at a certain page. When the act was over, Nancy, blinking in the light, again focused her eyes on the program.

Yes, there it was!

"—under the direction of Professor Emery Forsythe, Department of English, assisted by N. Smith Drew of the Avon Dramatic Company."

"Ned," Nancy whispered, "who is 'N. Smith Drew'?"

"Think she's a relative?" Ned smiled.

"Then it is a woman?" Nancy demanded.

"Yes, despite the masculine name," Ned replied. "Something like that girl friend George of yours. Miss Drew is the real coach of the play. She is fairly well known as a Shakespearean actress!"

"That's Nancy Drew!" Nancy cried to Ned's utter mystification.

"Your name—" he began, and then his memory quickened. "You don't mean the missing heiress?"

"I'm sure of it," Nancy declared, turning in her seat to Marion Hutchinson, and showing her the program.

" 'N. Smith Drew,' " Marion read. "Oh, do you think it can really be she?"

"It would be the most remarkable coincidence that ever happened if it turned out to be *the* Nancy Smith Drew," Nancy replied. "We must find her as soon as the play is finished."

Ned tried fruitlessly between the remaining acts to thread his way through the crowd to "back-stage."

"We'll have to wait until the play is over," he said at the beginning of the fifth act.

"I'm glad this isn't a real theater," Nancy said happily. "It ought to be easy to locate Miss Drew in this sort of a place."

When the last line was spoken the entire cast lined up in front of the audience, which arose and applauded vigorously. Ned and Nancy, swiftly joined by Marion, wasted no time in hand-clapping but forced their way forward.

"Oh, they are marching out!" Nancy cried. "Hurry, hurry!"

The players were walking out in a double procession, through small doors beneath the balcony of the gymnasium.

"I'll go to that side and you keep on this," Ned suggested. "Then we shall be sure to find her."

He vanished into the crowd.

The players had all disappeared by the time Nancy and Marion reached the row of metal-sheathed doors. Neither of the girls knew where they led.

"I think they went in here," Nancy said, pushing against one of the doors.

It opened, and the two girls found themselves in a small, metal-walled room that was utterly bare of furnishings. Opposite them was another door, and Nancy opened it to disclose a flight of metal steps that spiraled downward and up. A single unshaded electric bulb feebly illuminated the stair well.

"Up or down?" Marion asked.

"Let's go down first," Nancy suggested. "Or, to save time, I'll go down and you go up."

Gathering their dainty frocks in their hands the girls negotiated the stairs. Nancy went down to another door, which was pushed open, to be greeted by a furnace and a huge coal pile.

She turned and scurried back up the steps. Past the door where they had entered she ran and on up to the next landing, where she encountered Marion.

"We came in the wrong door," the Hutchinson girl said. "There's nothing up here but a big dark room and the stairs just continue to the roof."

"Then there is nothing to do but to try the next door," Nancy said with disappointment.

The two girls started to retrace their steps gingerly.

Nancy reached the door first and pushed against it. To her dismay it would not budge.

"Some one must have—must have locked it!" she stammered.

"Maybe there is a button to push," Marion said.

The surface of the door was as smooth as the wall into which it fitted. The girls knew that beyond them a noisy throng was preparing to dance, but not a sound reached their ears.

"Nobody will hear us knocking," Nancy cried. "We're trapped!"

CHAPTER XIX

Prisoners in Darkness

For a moment the two girls stared at each other in dismay, and then—the light went out!

"Oh!" cried Marion. "I'm afraid in the dark. Nancy, give me your hand!"

"I can't see you," Nancy replied. "Be careful that you don't slip."

She felt Marion's groping hand and seized it comfortingly.

"Let us feel our way down to the furnace pit," Nancy suggested. "Some one must be in charge there."

The girls groped their way down the steep iron stairs to the floor below. Except for the faint gleam from the open furnace door pitch darkness reigned.

"Hello! Anybody here?" Nancy called.

Not even an echo answered.

"Well, that's that," Marion said grimly. "Don't let go my hand, please, Nancy."

"Let's try the top floor. It isn't any darker there now than it is anywhere else," Nancy suggested.

Slowly the two felt their way up the spiral stairs, until they reached the second landing. Nancy groped for the door, which opened to her touch.

"I wonder what Clifford and Ned must be thinking," Marion said. "I told Cliff to sit just where he was, that I'd be back in a minute. The poor dear doesn't even know where I went."

"We'll be sorry-looking dancing partners if this place is as dirty as it smells," Nancy said, stepping cautiously into the blackness, with one hand stretched before her.

"If a mouse jumps on me I'll die," Marion declared. "And spiders—ugh!"

"After this I'll carry a flashlight with me wherever I go," Nancy said jokingly to take her new-found friend's mind off her fright.

"After this, I'll never go through a door without being certain of what is on the other side," Marion vowed.

"I think I see a light down there," Nancy said. "Wait a minute, there is something in front of us."

"Is it alive?" cried Marion.

"No, it's just a big box," Nancy said. "This must be a storeroom of some kind."

Nancy's guess was correct. The top floor of the gymnasium building was used as a place to store athletic equipment not being used, such as gymnasium apparatus, baseball uniforms and bats and protectors, hockey sticks and goals—in short, all the movable paraphernalia of a university's sports.

It was slow going. Every step of the way had to be taken slowly, with toes and fingers gingerly feeling for obstructions.

"I can see now," Nancy said. "There is a row of windows down here and the light from the street shines through them."

Eventually there was enough light admitted by the windows to permit the girls to walk less hesitatingly.

"My goodness, what poor housekeepers these men are," Nancy said. "Did you ever see such dirty windows?"

A few more steps and it was revealed that the windows were not dirty, but covered with a stout metal mesh.

"Oh, they must open somehow!" Marion cried.

Nancy's fingers searched around the edges of the iron screens.

"No luck," she sighed. "They are screwed into place."

"Oh, dear, we shall have to spend the night here," cried Marion, on the verge of tears.

Nancy was not one to admit defeat so easily. She tried each of the four windows in turn, and found them all securely fastened.

"I can't even figure out where we are," she exclaimed. "It certainly is not the front of the building."

She studied the ground below. The light came from a lamp attached to the building, and Nancy guessed it was over a door, for she could make out the crushed gravel of a driveway beneath.

Suddenly an automobile drove up directly under the window.

"Here's a car, Marion!" Nancy cried. "We'll be able to attract somebody's attention."

Marion came close to the screened window and looked down.

"And there is somebody coming out of a door," she said. "Call out!"

The two girls beat against the screening and shouted at the top of their lungs.

A woman wearing an evening wrap, with a scarf thrown over her hair, was being assisted into the automobile by a top-hatted man. They both looked around them as they heard the faint sounds that came to their ears from the imprisoned girls above them.

"She sees us!" Nancy cried, as the woman looked up at the windows.

To the horror of the girls, however, the woman merely waved as if acknowledging a greeting, and vanished into the car. The man stepped in behind her and the despairing prisoners saw the car dash away and disappear from view.

Marion slumped against Nancy's shoulder.

"I'm afraid I'll have hysterics," she said with a high-pitched little laugh. "Nancy, that was the girl you are looking for. That is Nancy Smith Drew—and now she is gone again, and here we are."

"If two persons came out of that door more will follow," Nancy said grimly. "Here, hold me up a minute."

Nancy leaned on Marion's arm and took off one of her new slippers.

"What are you going to do?"

"A little house-breaking, from the inside out," Nancy said. "And here are my thanks to the person who invented spike heels."

The high, narrow heel of the slipper passed easily through the coarse mesh of the window grating.

"The next person we see is going to get a shock," Nancy promised.

She held the slipper poised!

Minutes that seemed like hours dragged by. Nancy shifted the slipper to her left hand so she could rest her aching wrist. Then she transferred it to her right.

"I can't stand on one foot any more," she finally said. "Here's where a pair of good stockings is going to be ruined."

"Wait, here's my handkerchief—stand on that," Marion exclaimed, stooping and spreading the filmy square of fine linen on the dusty boards.

"Here comes somebody at last," Nancy cried, bringing the heel of her slipper down with all the force she could muster against the pane.

Crash!

The glass splintered beneath the blow, and its fragments tinkled on the hard ground beneath.

"Hi! What's the idea?"

"Who's up there?"

Two deep masculine voices roared up from below, as Nancy peered down through the hole in the window to see what results her stratagem had produced.

"Ned!" she cried. "Oh, I'm so glad it's you. We are locked in!"

"Nancy! Locked in! I'll have you out in a jiffy," shouted Ned.

"Is Marion up there with you?" his companion called.

"Here I am, Cliff!" Marion cried, her good humor immediately restored at the prospect of an early rescue. "What are you doing down there? Didn't I tell you to stay where you were sitting until I came back?"

"They picked the chairs up," Doolittle called back laughingly over his shoulder.

In a minute or two all the lights in the store-room were flashed on, and the pounding of feet on the iron stairs could be heard.

Nancy and Marion scampered toward the door, where they were met by Ned and Clifford.

"How in the world did you get up here?" the boys demanded in chorus.

"We followed—or thought we did—the actors through the door below," Marion explained.

"When we tried to get out it was locked," Nancy said, "and then the lights went out."

"We thought you had been kidnaped," Cliff growled.

"After going through the first door you should have turned right to the dressing-room door instead of going straight on through," Ned explained.

"Well, it's too late now," Nancy mourned. "We saw Miss Nancy Smith Drew—get away from us."

CHAPTER XX

The Thief's Lair

Marion and Nancy went to a dressing-room and removed the smudges they had accumulated on their fruitless quest.

The dance was well under way. The University Glee Club band was drumming forth the latest tunes, and the rhythm soon erased Nancy's disappointment. After all, the worst that had happened was a delay in finding Miss Drew.

At midnight the orchestra played "Home, Sweet Home," which had no effect on the dancers. Thereafter the musicians hopefully alternated the tune with each dance number, and at one o'clock solved their problem by packing up their instruments and walking off the floor.

In just such jolly and informal a way the dance came to a close. The men and boys lined up to claim their escorts' wraps at the cloakroom, and soon goodnights were said and Nancy was walking over the frozen ground abreast of Mr. and Mrs. Nickerson and Ned.

"Well, who's game to get up at six o'clock and take a ten-mile hike with me?" Mr. Nickerson asked laughingly.

His only response from the three others was a hollow groan.

"I thought—that is, if Nancy were willing—that we might remain here until after luncheon tomorrow to avoid the traffic jam," Mr. Nickerson continued.

"Of course I am willing," Nancy agreed, and then an idea flashed into her head.

"Ned," she said, "you run along like a nice little boy. I have something to tell your father in secret."

Ned was no more surprised than was his father as Nancy took the older man's arm and in a low voice earnestly told him a long story, the nature of which the others could not make out so easily.

Mr. Nickerson's occasional "Oh's" and "Aha's" and "I see's" made Ned squirm with curiosity.

"Of course I'll do it!" Mr. Nickerson said aloud as Nancy came to the end of her tale. "I think you are a most remarkable young woman. It will delight me to have a share in your adventure."

"But it is a secret," Nancy warned. "I know it is very discourteous to whisper in the presence of others," she explained to Ned and his mother, "but Mr. Nickerson and I have laid a deep, dark plot."

"Nothing could please him more," Mrs. Nickerson laughed. "I think he reads every detective story published, and he is always moaning that he cannot be partner to a 'deep, dark plot.'"

At the fraternity house Nancy bade her friends a final goodnight and went to her room. Helen had not yet returned, so Nancy quickly tumbled into bed and was fast asleep long before her roommate came in.

Again the tolling of the college chimes awakened her. Helen opened one sleepy eye and then ducked under the blankets as Nancy arose and dressed.

"Shut the windows, please," came in muffled tones from beneath the covers of the occupied bed. Nancy obligingly closed the casements, made sure the steam radiator was turned on, and went downstairs.

The colored porter was lounging on a chair in the hallway, a mop and duster beside him, reading a newspaper.

"Good morning," Nancy smiled. "I wonder if you have a road map of the State."

"Right in de room dere," the porter said with a wave of his hand. "Day's a whole slew ob dem in dat desk, Miss."

Nancy helped herself to the required map

and pored over it, tracing routes with her finger.

"Good morning! Look's like a grey day!" boomed a voice from the doorway. Nancy looked up and saw Mr. Nickerson.

"Have you had breakfast?" he asked. "No? Neither have I. Suppose we stop at a restaurant, and you can tell me more in detail something about this quest we are on."

The sleek sedan was at the door, and Nancy sat down beside Mr. Nickerson as he drove away and headed for the main street of the town. He parked in front of a restaurant, in which he and Nancy found themselves to be the only customers.

"How about some orange juice, buckwheat cakes with country sausage and coffee?" Mr. Nickerson asked, studying the menu. "Homely but substantial. Or are you one of these modern young women who breakfast on dry toast and hot water?"

"Not at all," Nancy laughed. "I'll even add an order of buttered toast to that, but change the coffee to cocoa."

While waiting for breakfast, and during the eating of it, Nancy told Mr. Nickerson at length the story of the stolen mail pouch and her suspicions as to the culprit.

"This Edgar Dixon lives in Stafford, which is just twelve miles up the river," Nancy explained. "I remember the address Mr. Dixon gave me. If he were at the game yesterday he must still be living near here. At least, we'll find out something about him."

A fine snow, hard and white and tiny as granulated sugar, was hissing down through the leafless trees when they emerged from the restaurant.

"A young woman as capable and self-reliant as yourself must be a wonderful driver," Mr. Nickerson said, pausing at the car door. "You know the road to Stafford. Wouldn't you like to drive?"

"I have never driven a car of this make," Nancy said. "But if you will risk the car——?"

"I have less worry with you at the wheel than if I were driving," Mr. Nickerson urged.

Nancy accordingly seated herself at the wheel, studied for a moment the way the pedals and levers worked, and then started off.

Driving was made difficult by the snow, which blew against the windshield and heaped up little drifts in the road.

"I hope we shan't have a blizzard," Nancy said. "Perhaps it would be best if I abandoned this idea and we started for home."

"Nonsense," Mr. Nickerson said. "If it comes to that we can put the car aboard a steamer and go home by boat."

Because of the uncertain road conditions and Nancy's caution with a strange car, it was forty minutes before they reached Stafford.

That community was a lumber town, dominated by the great saw and planing mills along the river, which every spring bore thousands of logs down on its swollen currents from the forests to the north.

At what was evidently the main four corners of Stafford Nancy stopped the car and inquired where Harrison Street was.

The policeman described the turns for her.

"Do you know where the Hemmers live?" Nancy asked.

"Sure thing," the policeman replied. "You can't miss it. It's the only red brick house on the street."

With these unmistakable directions Nancy soon had the car parked in front of the Hemmer homestead, its identity made certain by a sign in the window which read, "Hemmer House. Meals and Rooms by the Week," and in another window, "Furnished Room Vacant."

"I'll just stay in the background," Mr. Nickerson said, as Nancy dismounted.

She climbed up the steps which had once been swept of the snow, but were already whitened again.

Just as Nancy put out her hand to ring the bell the door opened and a ruddy-faced man with a bag slung over his shoulders, opened the door.

"Hello!" he exclaimed.

"Good morning," Nancy smiled. "I came to inquire for Mr. Dixon—Edgar Dixon. Is he here?"

"Dixon. Hmm!" frowned the man. "I think he left when his week was up Sunday. Wait, I'll ask the wife."

He craned his head and bawled. "Emma!"

In response to the summons a middle-aged woman, plump and pleasant-faced, came to the door.

"Why do you keep the young lady standing in the snow, John?" she asked. "Ain't you got any manners at all? Come in, Miss."

"Just for a minute, then," said Nancy, already convinced her trip was a failure. She stepped into the hall, John Hemmer following and shutting the door.

"She's looking for Dixon," he explained to his wife.

"You ain't the young lady he's going to marry?" Mrs. Hemmer asked anxiously.

"Oh, no," Nancy laughed. "I'm just a friend of his older brother, who is sick in bed."

"That's too bad. I hope you didn't come far," Mrs. Hemmer said. "No, Mr. Dixon left here Sunday. He gave me a week's notice. He said he had come into a fortune and was going to get married. I was sorry to lose him. He was a real nice gent, except that he got an awful lot of mail and wrote enough letters to fill a book every day."

"Do you know where he went?" Nancy asked.

"No, he didn't say," the boarding-house mistress answered.

"He gave me this elegant leather bag to carry my tools in," Mr. Hemmer chimed in. "I'm a carpenter. I was just going out on a job."

He displayed the leather pouch he carried. Nancy suppressed the exclamation that rose to her lips. She had seen that pouch a hundred times before. It was certainly Ira Dixon's mail bag!

Her hunch, her deductions, were justified. Edgar Dixon was the thief!

Mrs. Hemmer excused herself, and returned in a minute with a thick packet of letters in her two hands.

"I've been wondering what to do with all this mail," she said. "It's for Mr. Dixon. Not many of 'em has a return address, so I wonder if you would give them to him next time you see him?"

"Oh, but I don't know when—" Nancy began.

"Well, give them to his brother to keep, like a good girl," Mrs. Hemmer insisted. "I'm just worried about them. Here, take them, please.''

She thrust the bulky collection of letters into Nancy's hands.

''Well, thank you for your trouble,'' Nancy said, eager to leave before any other duties were forced upon her.

''Goodbye,'' the Hemmers said cheerfully.

Nancy descended the snowy steps cautiously, and at the foot stopped to smile at Mr. Nickerson. She was amazed to see a look of horror leap into his face, while simultaneously she heard Mr. Hemmer shout, ''Look out, Miss!''

The next thing Nancy knew she was sprawling in the snow. A sled, on which two small boys had been coasting, had run into Nancy and then had spilled its two young occupants into the snow.

Nancy was unhurt and quickly regained her feet. The little boys, badly frightened and stammering apologies, scooped up the scattered letters which were soaked with snow. Several of them had been cut almost in two by the sharp runners of the sled.

The lads shook the snow off the envelopes and handed them to Nancy.

''Oh! Money—don't lose it!'' Nancy cried out in surprise.

From the cut envelopes dollar bills were showering upon the snow-covered sidewalk!

CHAPTER XXI

EDGAR'S TRUE COLORS

"ARE you hurt, Nancy?"

Mr. Nickerson had jumped from the car and was brushing the snow from the dazed girl's coat.

"I—I don't know yet," Nancy said. "Look at the letters. Mrs. Hemmer gave them to me to take to Edgar Dixon's brother until he called for them, and they are blurred and cut."

The two small boys crept quietly away, and as soon as they had put a few yards between themselves and Nancy they broke into a run, overcome by their feeling of guilt.

"Never mind the letters," Mr. Nickerson said. "The accident can be explained. How are you?"

Nancy took a step forward, and a twinge of pain flickered across her face.

"I must have twisted my knee," she said.

"You had better sit in the back seat," Mr. Nickerson advised. "I will drive back to Emerson."

She was carefully assisted into the roomy

rear seat and Mr. Nickerson put the bundle of torn and wet letters into her lap.

"That chap must have been running a mail-order business," he commented.

He began to maneuver the car to make a turn in the narrow street in order to head it back toward Emerson. The two small boys crept back cautiously to recover their sled, and seeing that they were not going to be molested, approached more boldly. The glitter of the big automobile seemed to fascinate them, and they stood staring, open-mouthed, on the curb.

A second car approached. That was a distinction for Harrison Street—two big, new cars visiting its narrow, old-fashioned length at one time.

Just as Mr. Nickerson completed his turn and was shifting from reverse to low speed, the other car halted in front of the Hemmer home. There were two men in the front seat.

Alertly Nancy lowered the window and looked out at the two. They were utter strangers to her.

"Hey, kid, does E. Dixon live here?" one of the men called to the boys.

The youngsters nodded.

As the automobile carried her away from the scene Nancy just barely heard the speaker cry out to his companion, "We're on the right trail of that scoundrel, Buddy!"

Mr. Nickerson's driving was not of the best. The car swayed and slipped in the packed snow, and the letters went hurtling from Nancy's lap in all directions. Some of them, so soaked that the flaps became loosened, and others that were cut by the sled runners, fell open and each shed its creased dollar bill and folded sheet of note paper.

Nancy began picking them up.

"I'll never in the world get them into their right envelopes," she thought, "but I guess that makes no difference."

She slipped the letters into the torn wrappers, but to make sure that some of them would not have two of the dollar bills inside she unfolded the note paper. Her eyes glanced over the writing without curiosity, for Nancy had been taught that mail is a personal thing and unless specific permission is given, it is to be left strictly unread by anyone but the addressee.

After re-folding the third or fourth sheet Nancy became aware that the salutation on each had been the same, and that it was certainly a most unusual one. Each letter had been addressed, "Dear Guide."

"Edgar Dixon cannot have been up to any good," Nancy assured herself, as she unfolded another sheet of note paper, noticing that this one had not lost its dollar enclosure.

Deliberately she read the letter:

"Dear Guide: Here is my dollar for the December dues. The letters you forwarded me from 'Sonora Joe' are beautiful. I think he is a lovely fellow and it is too bad he is going to lose his cattle because he cannot pay the interest on his mortgage. I am so glad I met him through the Lonesome Hearts Friendship Club. If you think it is all right I would like to send him $10 to help him along."

The letter was signed "Posy," and underneath was appended the real name and address of the writer.

Convinced that she had stumbled upon evidences of a base fraud, Nancy had no hesitation in reading another of the letters.

The writer of this, also a woman, had likewise enclosed a dollar for the December "dues," and must have been an older member of the "Lonesome Hearts Friendship Club," for she too, proved to be a benefactress of "Sonora Joe."

Nancy read:

"The last letter I sent you to forward to 'Sonora Joe' contained a small contribution to help him out of his trouble. He wrote me a beautiful reply in which he said he was so glad that Luck had given me to him as his correspondent in the Club, instead of one of the hundreds of other members. I know it is against the rules but I would like to know 'Sonora Joe' in person. Perhaps I could help him more substantially."

Nancy felt a surge of anger within her.

"This scoundrel of an Edgar," she murmured. "He must have been making a lot of money out of his fake correspondence club, working on the sympathies of lonesome, trusting women! Ugh! What a cad he must be."

On an impulse she asked Mr. Nickerson to stop the car as she wished to consult with him.

"I couldn't help but see what was written on one of these notes," she explained, "and what I saw made me suspicious, so I read another. Won't you read these two and tell me what you think of them?"

Mr. Nickerson perused the two letters, and as he read them a frown gathered on his brow.

"The man is a scoundrel of the deepest dye," he said as he finished. "If Uncle Sam discovers this, Dixon will be sent to a federal prison for a long term. Undoubtedly he was using the mails to defraud and victimize the members of a 'friendship club' of his own invention."

"That is exactly what I deduced," Nancy said. "I think, with this evidence, that Edgar will not bother his half-brother any more."

Mr. Nickerson regarded Nancy with frank admiration.

"You certainly have a genius for deduction," he said. "And you are generous, too, in the way you use it, Nancy. I must voice my admiration for you! Your father is a fortunate man to have such a splendid daughter!"

Nancy blushed a deep red. The hearty praise embarrassed her. She did not know how to reply to such words.

Mr. Nickerson, with a final smile, put the car into motion again and before long the towers of Emerson came into view.

At the hotel Mrs. Nickerson and Ned were just finishing their breakfast, while at an adjoining table Helen and her mother and Buck and his parents were in the middle of theirs.

"Here are the early birds!" Ned cheered, as Nancy and Mr. Nickerson found them in the dining room.

"The weather is pretty cold for worms, though, even for the earliest of birds," Mrs. Nickerson laughed. "Did you catch any?"

"We caught the champion worm of—" began Mr. Nickerson, but Nancy laid a finger to his lips.

"Sh!" she cautioned. "No one must know, yet. The fewer who are in on the secret the better, you know."

"You can have your old mysteries," Ned laughed. "Just look how hard it is snowing. Who wants to go skiing?"

"I'm sorry, but I've hurt my knee," Nancy said. "Otherwise I'd love to go."

Everyone was most concerned about Nancy's injury, but she refused to take it seriously.

"It's nothing at all," she protested. "But I don't dare put my weight on it. Please forget all about it."

Secretly Nancy was glad of the excuse her sprained knee gave her, for she was laying plans for the entrapment of Edgar Dixon and the locating of the English Nancy.

CHAPTER XXII

At Professor Forsythe's

As soon as Nancy could get Ned conveniently aside she asked him to guide her to Professor Forsythe's house.

"Your father was good enough to take me out on a little detective work," she confided to Ned. "You understand, don't you, that I'd rather keep my plans secret until they materialize?"

"Anything you do is all right with me," Ned smiled. "If you want me to dress in feathers and war paint and play the Scotch bag-pipes up and down Main Street, I'll do it without asking you why!"

"Oh, Ned, you're such a good sport," Nancy laughed, convulsed at the picture of the football hero in mixed masquerade. "No, all I want you to do is to take me to the professor's house. He can tell me where the English Nancy is staying. She must still be in town."

Ned donned his overcoat and galoshes, and plunged into the snowstorm with Nancy.

"It isn't far," he said. "We can walk. Oh,

I forgot about your knee, though. We'd better ride.''

"I think perhaps the exercise will do it good," Nancy assured him.

It was but a short block and a half from the hotel to Professor Forsythe's home.

A youthful housemaid admitted the pair, and went to announce their presence to the professor, who was reported to be in his study correcting some papers. She returned with the invitation for the young people to enter the room at once.

Professor Forsythe rose from his desk to greet Ned and to be introduced to Nancy.

The study was lined with bookshelves from floor to ceiling, and the flat top of one of the biggest desks Nancy had ever seen was piled high with additional books and sheaves of papers.

"I want to tell you first of all how much I enjoyed the play last night," Nancy said. "I have never before seen one put on in the tradition of the Elizabethan theater, and I liked every minute of it."

Professor Forsythe bowed gravely.

"The credit is not mine," he said. "I taught the players their lines, but the artistry of the performance is all due to my associate, Miss Smith Drew. Is she a relative of yours by any chance?"

"No," said Nancy. "And there lies the real reason for my visit, Professor. I wish to meet Miss Drew to give her some important information that reached me instead of her because of our names being identical."

"I can tell you where she is stopping, although I believe she is planning to leave Emerson today or tomorrow," Professor Forsythe said. "She has a room at Mrs. Broderick's—you know where Mrs. Broderick's place is, Ned? It is that big, old mansion on Chapel Street where some of the instructors and junior professors board."

"I know the place, all right," Ned said.

Nancy, her heart high at the certainty she was at the end of one of her quests, made her adieus to the professor. With old-fashioned courtesy the man of learning escorted his young guests to the door.

"My gracious, what a storm," he exclaimed. "It looks like a blizzard. I don't think the afternoon boat will sail, if this keeps up. It is blinding."

"I'm sure Father won't drive home in this weather, either," Ned remarked. "He'd get snowbound in the country."

"Shall we go around to the Broderick place?" Ned inquired, as they left the house.

"I'd like to, very much," Nancy replied. "Of course, there is no great hurry. We have until this afternoon, at least. Do you want to go, Ned?''

"Just say the word," the youth declared. "I will go get Father's car if you are tired from tramping through the snow."

"I don't think I can walk much farther," Nancy said. "Not because my knee hurts, but you see I didn't expect the snow, and I have no rubbers."

"Here, pull on these galoshes," Ned ordered. "I guess you can get both feet into one."

"Oh, I wouldn't do that," Nancy protested.

A loud whoop interrupted their friendly debate, and they turned to see a knot of young men coming toward them dragging a bob-sled.

"Just in time," Ned called out. "Here, I have a passenger for you, fellows."

The youths, all college students, gallantly halted and insisted upon Nancy seating herself on the sled.

"Going anywhere in particular?" one of them asked. "How about one slide down Citadel Hill?"

"Glorious!" exclaimed Ned. "You'll love it, Nancy. Have you time?"

Nancy was really eager to get to the boarding house where Miss Drew was stopping, but she felt that courtesy demanded she accept the invitation.

With a whoop the boys started off on a trot,

easily dragging the long double-runner sled to which Nancy clung. The snow fell unceasingly, and it was an exhilarating ride.

"Citadel Hill," explained Ned, as he walked along beside Nancy, "is the only hill worth the name in town. When this was a frontier trading town there was a fort on the hill as a protection against the Indians. That's how it got its name. You'll enjoy the view, if you can see anything in this snow."

It was nearly a mile tramp to the summit of the hill, down which other sledding parties were skimming with shouts of delight from the boys and cries of alarm from the girls as the bobs flew down at express-train speed. Nancy saw Helen flash by on a sled guided by Buck.

From the summit of the hill Ned pointed out the direction of the river, the wharf, and other quarters of the town, all of which were concealed by the blinding snow.

Then, with the coast clear, the boys piled on the sled. Sturdy feet pushed it along until it gained momentum on the decline. Slowly at first, then faster and faster, the long bob slid over the crisp snow. Soon everything was a blur before Nancy's eyes as the sled picked up speed. The snow struck her cheeks with the force of sharp gravel hurled by an unseen hand, and the runners sang like a bow continuously drawn over the A string of a violin.

At the foot of the hill the bob sped along for more than a hundred yards before it slid to a halt.

"That was as thrilling as an airplane ride," Nancy cried.

"What about an encore?" the boys shouted, and without further ado wheeled about and began the long climb to the hilltop again.

Once more the meteor-like rush down the long slope, and at the conclusion of that ride Nancy begged to be excused.

"On to the hotel, then," cried one of the students, who had been in the play the evening before. "Never let it be said that Emerson youth turned fair lady out into the snow."

So, with all the display of an Empress of old Russia being returned to her castle, Nancy was delivered to the hotel on the sled pulled by half a dozen young men. She thanked each one individually.

"Say, I'm just about starved from the exercise and the cold," Ned confessed, as he opened the hotel door for Nancy.

"Well, I'm rather hungry myself," she laughed. "Remember, I had my breakfast before you were even up and about."

As she entered the lobby Nancy was electrified to hear a bellboy paging her—or was it the English "Miss Drew—Miss Nancy Drew, please," that was being sought?

CHAPTER XXIII

SNOWBOUND

"No MATTER which Nancy, I'll answer the call," the girl decided.

She signaled the page.

"Miss Nancy Drew?" he asked. "Telephone call, please. In Booth No. 1."

Tipping the lad for his service, Nancy entered the designated booth and picked up the receiver.

"Hello?" she said, half hoping the message would be for the English Nancy so she could obtain a further clue.

"Hello, Nancy, this is your father," came the familiar voice of Carson Drew. "I'm glad to hear that Mr. Nickerson did not start out in the blizzard. I am on my way to Emerson."

"Good! I'm pining for a look at you," Nancy laughed. "You are the most elusive parent anybody ever owned!"

"Don't flatter yourself," Mr. Drew said with mock severity. "I am not coming to see you, but to consult with Dean Snyder."

"Who is he?"

"He is Dean of the Law School at the University," Mr. Drew explained. "I want to consult him on some obscure points in the land laws of the State."

"Where are you now?" Nancy asked.

"I'm at a garage about fifteen miles from Emerson, getting a new set of chains put on the car," her father replied. "The links on one chain wore through on the way up.

"However, that isn't what I telephoned you for. On the chance of meeting you on the road or of your staying over at the college, I brought a cablegram that came to the house for you."

"From the English lawyers?" Nancy asked.

"Yes. It says, in effect, that they thank you very much for your offer to help find the real heiress, that they will make good any expense you incur, and they hope you will locate her soon because they would like to get rid of the responsibility of her estate. In United States money it's worth about $75,000."

"You will scarcely believe it, Dad, but who do you think I learned is in town here?" Nancy asked.

"The English Nancy, I suppose?" Mr. Drew replied.

"Yes, how did you guess it?" Nancy cried.

"You aren't joking? Why, I guessed that in fun," Mr. Drew exclaimed. "Have you seen her yet?"

"I will this afternoon," his daughter replied confidently.

"I'll be there in less than an hour," her father replied. "I'd be there in twenty minutes but the roads are all but blocked by drifts. Goodbye, then."

When Nancy stepped from the booth she saw that the Nickersons were waiting for her before going in to luncheon. She told them that her father was coming to Emerson, and his reason for doing so.

"He says the roads are all but impassable," Nancy added.

"What's more," Mr. Nickerson commented, "the afternoon steamer won't leave until tomorrow morning, because of an ice jam down the river. So it looks as if we should be marooned here, at least for another night."

While Ned escorted his mother to the table, Nancy, following with Mr. Nickerson, told him of the cablegram.

The four were ushered to a table near the windows, affording a view of the main street, practically deserted because of the snowstorm. Only rarely did anyone pass on foot or in an automobile.

Nancy was in the middle of her meal when, from the corner of her eye, she saw a pedestrian pass the window, head bent low before the storm. Some unexplainable sixth sense made her look up, just in time to catch a glimpse of a familiar yellow overcoat!

"Oh!" Nancy exclaimed involuntarily.

"What is the matter?" Ned asked. "You look as if you had seen a ghost."

"I almost did," Nancy replied cryptically. She wondered if she would be thought queer if she jumped from the table and ran out to follow the man.

"Well, if he is in town he can't get out," she thought with satisfaction. Aloud she said:

"Ned, you can see the lobby from where you are sitting. Watch to see if a man with a loud, yellowish overcoat comes in."

With a puzzled look in his eyes Ned kept watch a few minutes.

"No one has come in at all," he said. "What's the idea?"

"Someone passed whom I know—or think I know," Nancy replied with a careless air. "It doesn't matter."

"I think you are the most mysterious person I ever met," Ned said, viciously stabbing at a morsel of veal cutlet. "You even have Father walking around looking like a sphynx."

"I hope I don't look as old as that," Mr. Nickerson chaffed. "At least, I have all my nose and my feet."

"You'll need them," Ned said solemnly. "Before long Nancy will have you using your nose to track down crooks like a bloodhound.'"

The conversation took on a joking tone, and the meal was finished in high spirits.

"May I use the car, Father?" Ned asked. "I am going to drive Nancy around to her namesake's boarding house."

"Certainly, Son," Mr. Nickerson replied. "I hope your excursion with Ned has the great results our partnership produced," he added, turning to Nancy.

The boarding house where Nancy was driven by Ned a few minutes later was a wide, three-story brick structure, evidently remodeled from a mansion of pre-Civil War days. Ned explained that it had once been the sumptuous home of a lumber baron, but when the industry had moved farther up the river it had changed hands several times and was now the best rooming-house of the town.

"A number of the instructors and junior professors board there," Ned offered. "It is more like a hotel than a rooming-house, really."

With high hopes of success, Nancy walked up the path and rang the doorbell. A colored maid appeared and admitted her.

"My name is Miss Drew," Nancy said. "I am looking for another Miss Drew—Miss N. Smith Drew—who is stopping here, I believe?"

"Yas mum," the maid answered. "Miss

Drew, she done gone out. Ah'll ask Mis'
Broderick when she expect her back."

Mrs. Broderick herself entered the room to
explain matters to Nancy.

"Miss Drew," she smiled, "has gone out to
do some last-minute shopping, for reasons I
expect you will understand. I really do not
know when she will return. I know she planned
to be late because she wanted to purchase a
coat and to remain at the shop until it was
altered to fit, if necessary."

"Thank you, I will come back later in the
day, or probably tomorrow morning," Nancy
said, her hopes dashed again.

"I suppose you are a relative come to attend
the marriage," Mrs. Broderick said, as Nancy
left the house. "I'll tell her you were here."

"Thank you," said Nancy, too bewildered to
deny the relationship.

Marriage?

"Did you hear Miss Drew was planning to
get married?" she asked Ned. "She isn't
home—she has gone out to complete her
trousseau at the last minute."

"I know nothing about it," Ned replied. "I
sort of had the impression she was so much in
love with William Shakespeare no other man
could ever interest her," he added laughingly.

"Will you take me around again tonight, or
tomorrow morning?" Nancy asked.

"I certainly will," Ned promised.

Back at the hotel Nancy and Ned found Marion Hutchinson and the full-back, Doolittle, together with Helen, Buck and several other young couples discussing ways and means of spending the afternoon. Various games were suggested and rejected.

"Why not have a masquerade party to-night?" Nancy asked. "We could use up the afternoon making costumes out of the clothes we brought along."

"A great idea!" chorused the others. "Three cheers for Nancy Drew!"

"That will be a real challenge of ingenuity," Marion declared. "The rules are that sheets and pillow-cases from the hotel are barred, otherwise all the boys will dress as ghosts and Roman senators."

The young people scattered to plot and scheme. Nancy waited in the lobby for her father.

At last, well over the hour he had figured necessary to spend in completing the journey, Carson Drew entered the hotel. Except for the little arc on the windshield kept clean by the automatic wiper, the car was plastered with snow.

"It's getting warmer, and the snow is softer," he said, stamping and shaking himself to knock off the clinging flakes.

Mr. Drew gave Nancy the cablegram, while she explained her first fruitless visit to the boarding-house.

"At any rate, she is in town with little likelihood of leaving," Nancy concluded. "That will be one mystery solved. On top of that I am hot on the scent of Edgar Dixon——"

Thereupon she related to her father her suspicions concerning the man in the yellow overcoat.

"And that recalls something that nearly slipped my mind," Mr. Drew exclaimed. "I had a telephone call from Ira Dixon. He was trying to get in touch with you. He said he had come to the conclusion you had misjudged his half-brother, who seems to be trying earnestly at his own expense to catch the man who took the mail-bag, and so Ira wrote to him offering him a share of his fortune."

Nancy bit her lip in vexation.

"Edgar Dixon is a crook and I have the evidence to prove it," she asserted. "He has been using the mails to defraud women with a fake Friendship Club. Mr. Nickerson drove me to Stafford where Mr. Dixon just gave up his quarters, and I came into possession of letters which prove what I have said."

Mr. Drew looked at his daughter with wonder and admiration in his eyes.

"I thought you came up here to see a football game," he said. "Instead, you seem to have been working overtime as a sleuth."

"It's all just good luck," Nancy smiled.

"But one must be keen to recognize good luck when it happens," Mr. Drew declared. "Everybody in the world has good luck, but few can recognize it. And now I must get busy. Enjoy yourself, Nancy dear, and more 'good luck' to you."

Mr. Drew inquired at the hotel desk as to which road would be best to reach the town where the State University was located, then kissed his daughter affectionately, and with a warning from her to drive carefully, got his overcoat.

"I'll be back here for dinner," he called, "and then, if it is still snowing, I shall probably get a room for the night."

"We are going to have a masquerade," Nancy said. "Ned has put a notice on the bulletin board inviting all the hotel guests to join. Can't you invent a costume and come?"

"I'll be giving an imitation of a book-worm, if I can get the books from the legal library I hear the Dean owns," Mr. Drew said, as he stepped out of the door.

As Nancy bade her father goodbye at the Inn doorway, she saw a car go past somewhat jerkily. Apparently the driver was having engine trouble as the machine labored along the roadway. The driver's appearance gave her a start.

"Of course," she thought, "there surely are lots of yellow sports coats in this state, but somehow there is a familiarity about the wearer, too. Could it be Edgar Dixon? I *must* follow and see!"

Quickly Nancy raced to the Hutchinson suite, where she had left her coat and hat. Marion was there. She had decided to dress as a Hindu princess, with the aid of many scarfs and her plentiful supply of jewelry.

"That's my cue," Nancy cried. "I'll be a Hindu prince and your escort at the party to-night."

"But where are you going now?" inquired Marion curiously as she beheld Nancy donning her fur coat with all possible speed.

"I just have to see a man," explained the attractive girl somewhat hastily. "I'll tell you later all about it!"

"I'm rather surprised. Really, must you see a man—er, now, alone?"

Nancy laughed back over her shoulder.

"Do not worry—it's important, and I'll be all right."

She hurried along the snowy streets of the town, but could not see the car, nor hear its sputtering engine.

"Goodness," she muttered, "I don't wish

anybody trouble a day like this, but **Edgar**
Dixon has caused other people so much trouble,
he deserves some himself. I hope his old car
does break down and I can catch him!''

On and on the brave, determined girl hurried, thinking of old, gentle Ira Dixon, believing
his step-brother only a "wild boy," when in
reality he was such a scoundrel.

The snow was coming down harder now, and
it made Nancy breathless as she hastened her
steps. A turn brought her up short. Should
she go to the right or to the left? Which direction had the driver in the yellow overcoat
taken?

Nancy hated to be foiled, but after all, it did
seem useless to follow on foot, for if the driver
had nursed the engine into a better rhythm, he
would by this time have the automobile at least
a mile away. So Nancy gave up the chase for
the time being, returning more slowly to the
Inn and to the excited girls who were preparing
for the evening masquerade.

Nancy at once caught the spirit of the fun,
and began work on her own costume. Since
she had suggested the fancy dress party, she
felt that she should take great pains with her
own attire. Her efforts were well rewarded,
and she was a picture as she joined the merry-
makers that evening.

It was a harlequin crowd that gathered in the

ball room of the hotel after dinner, where a phonograph manned by a grinning waiter had been moved to substitute for the non-existent band. There were pirates and Indians galore, fat men, Siamese twins, bandits and black-face characters. One enterprising youth had taken advantage of his small stature and had induced a waitress to lend him her black-and-white uniform, frilly apron and all.

To make matters more exciting the hotel had donated prizes—books and boxes of candy selected from the stand in the lobby—for the best costumes. There was a prize for the most ingenious costume, the funniest, and the most beautiful. Judges were selected from among the older people who came to watch, but did not care to participate in the masquerade.

When the time came to award the prizes Nancy was truthfully surprised to learn she had been selected the winner as having the most picturesque costume.

She had appeared in a turban of colored silk, with the feathers from her hat held in place in front with a large brooch. A tight crimson sash, actually a long tippet borrowed from Ned, held up baggy, ankle-length white bloomers and the short jacket of her green suit made her costume look authentic. She had darkened her eyebrows and lashes, which heightened the bizarre effect of her disguise.

"I protest that prize," spoke up a girl whom Nancy had not met, although she had seen her before in the lobby.

"On what grounds?" demanded the master of ceremonies, the manager of the hotel.

Nancy, deeply embarrassed, shrank back.

"Oh, if anyone is going to make trouble, please let me withdraw," she murmured, although puzzled at the objection raised in such an abrupt manner.

The envious girl, who had deliberately cut up one of her gowns into strips and tatters to appear as Cinderella, pointed at Nancy.

"The rules said that everything could be used except sheets and pillow-cases," she sneered. "And there's the person who proposed the masquerade violating the rule. Those trousers she has on are certainly made from nothing but a sheet and a few pins."

"I over-rule the protest," the master of ceremonies declared. "I happen to know—because I provided the material—that that part of the prize-winner's costume is made from a table-cloth."

Everyone in the place impulsively broke into applause—with the exception of the envious young lady who had provoked the scene. She turned and left the room with as much hauteur as she could summon.

Nancy merely laughed the situation off with

her usual good nature, helping an unpleasant scene to be soon forgotten.

"Ned," called the prize winner, "I guess I'm ready to leave. Will you carry my gorgeous five-pound box of sweets for me?"

The young man quickly accepted the candy with a low bow like a servant doing the Hindu Prince's humblest bidding.

The merry-makers were leaving the gayly bedecked ball room. Clifford and Marion were already as far as the archway of the long lounge, smiling happily.

As Nancy edged toward the door, she suddenly caught a fleeting glimpse of a man's face. The sharp nose, the sleek head! It must be Edgar Dixon!

"Could he have been masquerading here to-night?" Nancy asked herself. "Perhaps I have danced with that man and never knew it!"

Then he was gone.

CHAPTER XXIV

THE REVEALING CONVERSATION

WEDNESDAY morning dawned bright, clear and comparatively warm. The drip of thawing snow was heard everywhere, and there was a great bustle in the streets of Emerson as the snow-bound sports-lovers prepared to start for their various homes.

At the hotel a bulletin was posted notifying all prospective steamer passengers that the boat would sail at noon.

Carson Drew joined Nancy and the Nickersons for breakfast.

"Are you ready to start for home immediately, Nancy?" he asked. "When do you plan to leave, Mr. Nickerson?"

"Some time in the forenoon," Ned's father replied.

"Just give me a chance to see Miss Drew right after breakfast," Nancy begged.

"Suppose I wait until you have completed your case," Mr. Drew smiled. "Then we need not delay the Nickersons from leaving as soon as they wish."

"No, Sir!" laughed Mr. Nickerson, pounding the table with his fist. "I have been granted a small part in this mystery drama your daughter is directing and I want to be in at the finish, even if I eat my Thanksgiving dinner at a roadside stand!"

Nancy decided to waste no time. Immediately after breakfast Mr. Drew started for River Heights and Nancy, with Ned and Mr. Nickerson, drove to the Broderick house.

While the men waited in the car, Nancy once more mounted the steps of the converted old mansion and rang the bell. This time Mrs. Broderick herself opened the door.

"Oh, good morning," she said, recognizing Nancy. "I'm extremely busy, so you just run upstairs by yourself, won't you? Miss Drew is on the third floor, in the west room."

Nancy ascended the wide, curving staircase that led upward from the big center hall. In the fashion of its day the stairs curved up in a wide, sweeping spiral from ground floor to top. The wall flanking it was pierced at intervals with deep recesses in which statuary or large vases containing dried hydrangea blooms and cat-tails were placed.

When she was half way between the second and third floors Nancy suddenly heard a spirited conversation between a man and a woman.

"Oh, Edgar, this is all so different from

the way I had hoped and planned," the woman was saying.

Mention of the familiar name caused Nancy to pause and listen.

"I'm awfully sorry, Smith," the man's voice responded in oily tones. "I had to use most of my ready money to get a brother of mine out of disgrace. He stole some money from the Government, but I will get it back and also a share of the fortune I told you about. Listen, let me read you a letter I just received."

Nancy heard the crackle of paper being unfolded, and then the man's voice continued:

"The letter says, 'I shall see that you get every cent you spent in my behalf back with interest, and that very soon,' and further down he adds, 'I expect the estate to be settled within the week and you shall get your share, dear Edgar, immediately afterward.' Why, I'll be rich, Smith. Rich!"

"But if you had only consulted me, Edgar! I know, dear, that what is mine is yours and what is yours will be mine."

"There was no time," Edgar replied. "The telegraph office reported all passage sold on the *Mesopotamia,* so I had to grab the last two tickets on the earlier boat. In order to make it we shall have to leave on the noon steamer from here and catch the train at River Heights for Chicago. I had to pay cash for everything, so I used the money I got from the check you asked me to cash. You must trust my judgment in the matter."

"All right, Edgar dear, but it will be hard to explain to Mrs. Broderick that the wedding will not be held here this afternoon, but in New York later," the girl's voice answered.

"What do we care for the old woman?" Edgar cried bluffly. "You finish your packing and I'll see about payment from the man who's buying my car. I'll be right back."

"Perhaps you had better leave the tickets with me," the woman suggested.

"All right, here they are, all in one envelope," Edgar was heard to say. "The little cardboard ones are for the river boat. Goodbye, darling, for just a few minutes."

Nancy looked about her for a place of concealment, and quickly stepped into a niche and edged herself behind a statue of a Greek woman in flowing robes. Unseen by the hurrying Edgar, Nancy had an excellent view of that person as he dashed past her down the stairs, a smile of triumph on his thin, tight lips.

The familiar yellow camel's hair overcoat, the gray cap, the fox-like countenance—handsome but untrustworthy—Nancy took them all in as the exultant bridegroom-to-be leaped down the stairs two steps at a time.

"Oh, the cad!" Nancy said to herself. "Of

all the contemptible men, Edgar Dixon takes first prize. He must get his just desserts before this day is over!''

Cautiously surveying the lay of the land before emerging from her hiding place, Nancy saw above her the young woman for whom she had so generously searched, the English Nancy Drew.

Miss Drew was leaning on the balustrade, gazing blankly down the deserted stairs. She held in one hand an envelope which Nancy guessed to be the one containing the steamer tickets.

N. Smith Drew was a tall, slender woman of about twenty-eight or thirty, Nancy surmised, fair in the typical English fashion. She was dressed in a henna colored woolen dress, cut square at the throat, with long sleeves, and wore a necklace of dull green stones. Nancy thought what a medieval looking picture the actress made, as her head, crowned with braids of flaxen hair, was bent in sorrow and doubt.

Then the proud, firm chin quivered and a sob escaped from the woman's throat. Nancy saw her throw an arm over her eyes, as she stepped backward out of sight.

Nancy climbed from her hiding place and resolutely ran up the remaining steps to the third floor.

The west room was at the head of the stairs,

and Nancy guessed that the conversation she had overheard had been carried on in its open doorway.

The door was shut now, and as Nancy paused in front of it, her knuckles poised to rap, she heard muffled sobs coming from beyond it.

On second thought Nancy lowered her hand to the knob and turned it gently. She opened the door and stepped into the room.

CHAPTER XXV

Two Searches Ended

Nancy found herself in a large, high ceil-inged room. A half-packed steamer trunk, two strapped satchels, chairs piled with folded gar-ments, and a number of empty boxes sur-rounded by tissue and wrapping paper bespoke the anticipated journey.

Across the old-fashioned, high-backed wal-nut bed lay the English girl, face down, her shoulders shaking.

Nancy walked across and put a sympathetic hand on her shoulder.

"Miss Drew," she said, "won't you look up, please?"

The half-concealed head shook negatively.

"Go 'way," came the choked command.

"I have something important to tell you," Nancy urged. "Something that will change your whole life."

The actress raised her head, and propped herself on an elbow. Blinking back her tears she stared at Nancy in astonishment.

"Who are you, and what do you want?" she

demanded. "How dare you enter my room without knocking?"

"Please listen," Nancy said soothingly. "My name is Drew—Nancy Drew. I don't blame you for looking surprised, but because my name is the same as yours, our paths have crossed here.

"Miss Drew, a fortune is awaiting you in England and the lawyers for the estate have been searching all over for you."

The actress sat upright.

"What sort of nonsense is this?" she asked. "Who would leave me a fortune?"

"I will explain everything, and show you all the proofs," Nancy said. "But first I must tell you something just as important. Edgar Dixon is a crook. He is deceiving you. You must have nothing more to do with him."

Miss Drew leaped to her feet and confronted Nancy with clenched fists pressed to her bosom.

"Oh, what are you saying? What are you saying?" she wailed.

Nancy's own eyes filled with tears at the sight of the distressed and shocked woman.

"Edgar Dixon is a mail robber, and has also been making a living deceiving women and girls through a correspondence scheme," she said gently. "I am sorry to have to tell you this, but the proof is plain. He——"

Miss Drew's eyes closed and she swayed

backward. Nancy leaped forward and caught
the fainting woman, guiding the unconscious
form to the bed.

From a wash-basin in the corner Nancy
brought water and sprinkled it on the woman's
face. Then she rubbed the limp hands, and in
a minute Miss Drew sat up again weakly.

"Oh, what news, what news," she muttered.
"Unbelievably good news, unbelievably bad
news.

"You must prove all this," she cried with
new vigor, looking up at Nancy. "How can I
believe you? Ah, you have a good face, you
could not be playing a cruel joke on me."

Nancy sat down beside her namesake and put
an arm over the quivering shoulders.

"Here is a cablegram I just received from
the lawyers," she said. "That will prove half
my tale to you. And if you will come downstairs with me I will introduce you to a man
who will convince you of the rest."

Miss Drew read the cablegram. Then she
stood up determinedly and put on a coat, evidently a new one, and donned hat and gloves.

"Take me to this man," she said quietly.

Nancy led the way downstairs and out to the
waiting car.

"Miss Drew, these are my friends, Mr. Nickerson, Senior, and Mr. Ned Nickerson," she
said.

"I know Ned Nickerson by sight, and I certainly have heard his name mentioned a million times since the game Monday," Miss Drew said with a wan smile. "With such a familiar person to bear you witness, I begin to believe in you."

"Then sit here in the car with us," Nancy requested. "Mr Nickerson will tell you how and why we traced Edgar Dixon to his home in Stafford and what we found there."

Proud to be playing such an important role in the drama, although not certain just how important it was, Mr. Nickerson told of the visit to the Hemmer boarding house, of the bundle of letters and how they came to be opened, and what was in them.

Then Nancy told of Ira Dixon's cruel fate.

Miss Drew listened without a word until the stories were finished, her lips and cheeks ashen.

"It is convincing," she said. "It explains why Edgar did many things he refused to explain. I must get away from here before he returns. I never want to see him again."

Ned volunteered to bring down the suitcases, and Nancy went along to help in every way she could to complete the packing. Miss Drew led the way to her room, and hastily placed her remaining clothing in the trunk. She made a last-minute survey of the place to see that she had forgotten nothing, and then closed the door behind her and joined her new friends.

Downstairs she summoned the dumbfounded Mrs. Broderick and told her that a last minute change in plans had occurred. She settled her bill, left some money with the boarding-house mistress for the servants, and then, without another word of explanation, walked proudly out to the car.

"Will you take me to the boat, please?" she asked Ned. "An expressman will call for the trunk."

Ned started the car as Miss Drew sank back in the rear seat beside Nancy and covered her face with her gloved hands. Nancy turned to comfort the stricken woman.

Thus it happened that neither of them saw the breezy, self-confident Edgar Dixon, his suave features still wearing his conceited grin, rush into the Broderick house.

"Ned," Nancy said, "please drive to the hotel. We have lots of time, and I want to see if Marion Hutchinson is still there."

Ned obligingly headed for the hostelry, and arrived there not a moment too soon. A limousine stood outside, with a uniformed chauffeur holding the door open for Marion.

Nancy called to her, as Ned halted his car behind hers.

Marion waved and called back:

"Hello, Nancy. Any luck?"

"Here is your old friend," Nancy called back. "Miss Drew!"

Marion ran over to the Nickerson car, and thrust head and shoulders inside.

"Is it really Nanna Drew? Nanna, don't you remember me? I'm Marion!"

There was an affecting scene as the former governess embraced her pupil, whom she had not seen for so long.

Marion interrupted Miss Drew's queries about brothers and sister.

"I hear you are going to be wealthy," Marion cried.

"I can scarcely believe it," Miss Drew replied.

"Oh, but it is true, I know," Marion insisted. "Nancy, here, has oodles of proof, and besides, her father is one of the most famous criminal lawyers in the country, and he knows it to be true, too."

"Then that takes away the final doubt," Miss Drew said, as the color returned to her pale cheeks.

Marion had to leave, and Miss Drew had to catch the steamer, so the reunion was very short, yet withal a most happy one for its participants.

As Ned headed for the steamer dock Miss Drew began to talk with animation of her future plans in England. She was a far different woman from the dejected one Nancy had aroused from tears in the boarding-house bedroom.

The steamer, columns of smoke spiraling from its twin stacks, was just giving the fifteen-minute warning whistle as Nancy guided Miss Drew up the gangplank, Ned and Mr. Nickerson following with the hand-baggage.

"There's my trunk," Miss Drew pointed. "Oh, steward, where are cabins A3 and A4? I wish to keep the better one and redeem the ticket for the other."

While the steward led the way Miss Drew said to Nancy that "so long as Edgar used my money in buying the tickets I certainly have the right to cancel his reservation."

The young English woman hugged and kissed Nancy, tears streaming down her cheeks, as farewells were exchanged.

"We shall see each other again," Miss Drew vowed. "I owe all my new-found happiness to you."

The roar of the ship's siren sent Mr. Nickerson, Ned and Nancy scurrying for the gangplank. Just as they reached the head of it an agitated figure, his yellow overcoat awry, stepped on the lower end of it.

"That's Edgar Dixon, the scoundrel!" Nancy cried.

"That's enough for me," Ned said grimly,

and leaped down the gangplank as if he were charging an opposing half-back. His shoulder caught Edgar off balance and sent the villain staggering backward. With a yell of anger and surprise he sat down in the slushy mud on the dock.

The boatswain's whistle shrilled, and the gangplank was raised as the steamer drew away from the dock.

"Hey, wait for me! I've a stateroom—" yelled the anguished Edgar.

"Another boat in two hours," bawled a deck-hand from the departing steamer.

Edgar cast his gray cap on the muddy dock and stamped on it. Then he rushed up to Ned, his fists doubled.

"You did that on purpose," he raged, while a little ring of hangers-on gathered around, hoping to see a fight.

Nancy, her eyes blazing, stepped forward between them.

"Yes, he *did* do it on purpose, Edgar Dixon," she cried. "He did it to save one more poor woman from your scheming clutches."

The crook looked at Nancy, his jaw dropping.

Two men shouldered their way through the crowd.

"Edgar Dixon, hey?" one of them said, clasping that person's shoulder with a huge hand. "I was afraid we were too late."

"Who are you?" Edgar demanded, his voice faltering.

"An operative of the United States Secret Service," the man said, throwing back the lapel of his coat to disclose a badge. "And this is Inspector Hewitt of the United States Post Office. I arrest you for using the mails with intent to defraud!"

"And I charge him with stealing a bag of mail from a mail carrier at my home," Nancy declared. "And——"

Dixon turned on her with a snarl.

"What are you saying?" he roared. "I mailed all those letters back to their owners."

"And besides that," Nancy said calmly, "although you will note that he did not deny stealing the bag, Mr. Inspector, I have a large bundle of letters I unearthed which will prove that he used the mails to defraud many women with a fake correspondence club."

A profound silence fell over the crowd at the brave girl's statement. Dixon seemed to wilt for a moment.

"You are the first girl ever to get the best of me," he growled, shaking his sleek head vigorously. "You are smart, all right."

"I am glad I found you out," replied Nancy, looking him straight in the eyes.

"Come along now," the Secret Service man said, giving Edgar a gruff push.

That canny crook, Edgar Dixon, was not yet vanquished, however. With a wriggle and a bound he shook off his coat, leaving it in the hands of the officer. Before anyone could make a move he leaped across the dock in two bounds and plunged into the icy river.

"Watch him!" ordered the quick-witted Nancy Drew.

"Hi, stop him!"

The crowd rushed to the edge of the dock.

There were only a few ripples on the surface of the river to mark where Edgar had plunged.

"Oh, he—may drown!" Nancy cried, anxiously scanning the heaving water.

"If he's a good swimmer," one old wharf hand said, "there's a couple of miles of docks he can hide under along the bank. Better get a boat, Mr. Detective."

"Yes," urged the excited Nancy, "don't let him die that way!"

At her suggestion the officials began a search, but the daring Edgar Dixon had outwitted them.

"There is nothing more you can do," Mr. Nickerson said to Nancy. "Let us go. I have never in my whole life had such an exciting morning, and I can't stand much more."

Nancy was satisfied—the other Nancy was safe and happy, and old Ira would be free again. She identified herself to the postal inspector and pledged herself to turn over all the evidence she had against Edgar, then walked to the automobile with Mr. Nickerson and Ned.

"So that solves two mysteries with one shot, eh?" Mr. Nickerson commented, beaming upon Nancy. "I never saw a girl, or anybody, man or woman, to equal you!"

Nancy modestly said nothing, blushing a little beneath Ned's frankly admiring gaze.

When they reached the Inn, Mrs. Nickerson was awaiting them, eager to hear the whole story which the clever Nancy had brought to such a satisfactory finish. Finally the luggage was placed in the car, and the jolly group set its course toward home and a happy Thanksgiving.

It might be added that Edgar Dixon was never again heard from, and that Ira, exonerated of theft and only mildly reproved by the Government for carelessness, received his honorable discharge from the Postal Service as well as his pension and the whole of his inheritance, together with a fine token from his friends and neighbors.

And Nancy—well, as may be expected, it was not very long before she found herself again plunged deeply into another mystery. Her readers may decide for themselves whether or not they consider "The Sign of the Twisted Candles" a more baffling secret.

"Nancy," exclaimed the exuberant Ned to the girl beside him, as he drove the long, tan sedan over the hard road at a lively pace, "you're not sorry, are you, that Edgar Dixon isn't along?"

Nancy laughed up into the young man's gay eyes.

"But seriously," she added, "I hope that I shall be forgiven for mixing mysteries with glorious entertainment."

"You are—entirely," he chuckled. "It added spice to the party, didn't it, Father?"

"Any time I receive a baffling piece of mail," laughed the older man, "I'll know to whom to go for assistance."

Nancy waved the compliment aside.

"Most of all, I'm proud that I could send Nancy Smith Drew back to England happy. The answer to my mysterious letter was ideal."

THE END